Falling Embers

R.G. Westerman

ISBN-13: 978-0-9981850-6-4

Dedicated

to

Wayne Richardson

Prologue

I never thought I had much in common with the undead. Turns out I was wrong.

The fire consumes the building in front of me. Flames leap into the night sky, illuminating the valley before me teeming with monsters, drawn like moths to a candle.

All they want is to consume, without feeling or consequence. There are hundreds of them, if not thousands.
Undead, zombies, all shuffling forward, seeing nothing, feeling nothing, but seeking everything. That deep, seething drive, burning hot until snuffed out by the fires.

Even in their final moments, I feel their need calling to me, beckoning to walk among them as if my presence comforts them, as if my inherent humanity calls to what is left of theirs, just as their monstrous nature calls to mine.

But I only have eyes for the building in the distance, the funeral pier in the middle of a sea of undead.

She is in there. Dr. Donovan. Margaret. The woman I once called Mother. She is human. Just a normal, regular human, unlike them.

Unlike me.

The good doctor thinks of herself as the savior of this world, but she is mistaken. Standing over this carnage, I cannot help but compare it to the world I left behind. Back, beyond the mountains at the water's edge. It feels like a lifetime ago, but it has only been days since I've left SeaHaven.

How much I wanted to be there again, surrounded by laughter, warmth, friends. But it is too late for that now. I have already resigned myself to the idea that I will not be returning in this lifetime.

The flames leap into the sky, and erupting flurries of sparks drift to the ground around me. The fire calls to me, beckoning to the inevitable end. I take a step forward, walking alongside them, joining the death march of the undead.

One

I don't remember when the headaches first start. Sometime after our arrival at SeaHaven, when the caravan came and got us, like the cavalry.

We had been hiking for a day and a half. Eva tended to the children, most of whom had marched along brave and steady, handling the forest terrain as well as any of us. Some of the younger ones had been carried, sleeping on shoulders when they couldn't keep up.

The vehicles park along the center of the vacant, two-lane road, three cars and a couple of vans. The exhaustion in my body creeps up on me, threatening to collapse my legs out from under me. All I can see is the backseat of the car and the reprieve offered.

A woman exits the driver's side, greeting Simeon with an embrace. She has the same dark brown skin as him, the same warm, kind smile. They kiss briefly, but I see the relief on both of their faces at seeing the other.

Everyone divides up into the available vehicles. I pile into the back seat between Thorn and Marcus. Rose climbs in by the window. I close my eyes, resting my head against the seat.

We drive for hours. The thrum of the car's movement lulls me into half-sleep, the fatigue winning out. Even then, I sense the warmth of the others next to me, the movement forward into the unknown. The sun crests the horizon, leaving in its wake a brilliant orange stripe painted across the green sea of the treetops.

When I open my eyes, I find the sun well into the sky and my head resting on Thorn's steady shoulder. He smiles down at me, his eyes sleepy. I smile back, but only a little, a thin ache blooming at the base of my neck.

This close to him, I notice his clothes hold the faint scent of burnt leaves. Marcus sleeps with his tiny head resting against my forearm, his childlike breath steady against my arm. Rose sits next to me on the other side, her head leaning against the side of the window. She does not sleep but just stares at the passing countryside, her eyes glazed with fatigue.

Bright orange sunlight tinges the edges of the trees, giving everything an otherworldly glow. As we descend from the mountains, buildings and houses appear here and there. Sidewalks and faded billboards pass us by.

I start to see people, apparently going about their morning, walking along the sidewalks with ease, greeting each other with smiles. This must be what people look like when they live without fear, I muse to myself.

Simeon stirs from dozing in the passenger seat. He stretches and yawns, reaching over and patting Clarice on the leg. "Good morning," he murmurs in his warm island accent.

"Good morning, my love," she replies with a smile.

"I see we're nearly there."

"We are getting close, now. Maybe another half an hour at the most."

I sit up, taking in the atmosphere. The car has slowed down, and I'm able to take in more detail. The first thing I notice is the strange clarity in my head. The further away we get from the mountains, the less I feel of... them. Threads of their connection break off, releasing their hold from my mind.

I hadn't realized how strongly I'd been bound to them until now. All I had ever known, voices... No, not voices, so much as a pull, a weakening connection receding into the distance.

I realize with a small dawning, for the first time, I feel free. I guess that's what it's called. At least, I know I've never felt this way before.

The atmosphere in the car feels so quiet and peaceful. Part of me wishes I could stay in this tiny bubble of safety forever. The prospect of the new life ahead is just as frightening as what lies behind us in some ways. I briefly consider asking where we are going, but Simeon and Clarice are speaking quietly to each other and I don't want to interrupt.

The caravan slows, pulling into a large, empty parking lot, edged right up against the large swath of sand leading to the ocean's edge. Against the far corner, a number of tables and booths create a small marketplace.

A few people mill about, too far to acknowledge us. I noticed some of them glance our way, shielding their eyes to get a glimpse.

"We are here," Simeon says with aplomb. "Journey's end."

One at a time, we climb out of the car. The rest of the caravan pulls in behind us, everyone parking and filtering out of their vehicles. The younger children blink away their sleep; everyone stretches stiff limbs, leaning and reaching to get the kinks out from the long journey.

I cannot take my eyes away from the never-ending expanse of blue, beyond the swell of sand. The waves gently lap against the shore, rippling and dancing.

"What is that?" I mutter.

"That is the ocean," Simeon says in his rich Jamaican accent, as he stretches his arms overhead. His deep brown eyes sparkle with excitement at the sight of the water. "Isn't she beautiful?"

"Are you smiling?" Thorn says out of the blue, stepping

towards me. His eyes catch the angle of the sun, illuminating the green depths of his gaze.

"I suppose I am," I reply. I hadn't realized it.

"That's something new," he says. "You should try it more often. It looks good on you." He steps away with a half-smirk.

I realize we have plenty of time to explore, and my empty stomach demands my attention. The aroma entices me from the marketplace, and I decide to make my way in that direction.

Many of the people greet Clarice and Simeon, old friends returning from the journey. Everyone is relaxed and smiling, shaking hands, hugging, and laughing. So different, even from Eden's farm and the compound.

This community manifested from a different kind of world than the one in which I grew up. No zombies, no monsters, no tricks, no games.

The scent of roasted meat overtakes my senses. I can't recall the last time I've properly eaten. Some of the other members of the caravan make their way towards one of the booths, where the sound of sizzling meat fills the air. My mouth waters at the sight of it.

An old man with a cheery face and a sizable stomach moved two large spatulas around a large, flat surface, a slab of metal heated by the controlled fire underneath. He dishes out portions of shaved meat, potatoes, and onions, served on pieces of flatbread. The man fills each with a spoonful of the mixture, handing them out one at a time to the gathering persons.

I receive mine and eat it so fast I nearly miss the flavors. I relish each bite, another meal for which I did not have to hunt, fight, or steal. To my surprise, Rose hands me a second one just as I finish the last bite of the first. I lick the juices off my fingers and dig in.

"Thank you," I say. "I wonder what this meat is."

"It's so good," Rose says. "Who cares?"

"Gather around, everyone!" Clarice calls out. She and Simeon stand next to a large fire pit close to the water's edge. Everyone from the caravan makes their way towards them. I, at least, felt glad to have some direction. Glancing around, it is easy to see who is new by the wide eyes and lost expressions. I'm sure mine is no different.

We make our way to the circle of weather-worn stumps which double as seats, circling the dry logs in the center. I sit down on the sand between Thorn and Rose, then Alma and Marcus.

"Welcome everyone," Clarice's voice rings out over the upturned faces. "Welcome to SeaHaven. Let me be the first to introduce all of you to your new home. I'm sure you are all ready to relax and settle in. Has everyone had something to eat?"

A murmur of affirmations and satisfaction filters over the crowd in response, leading to a small applause. The cook, standing at the edge of the gathering, gives a small wave of acknowledgment along with a cheery blush.

"Good, good," she says with a smile. "Everyone here comes from somewhere else, and we are all survivors. SeaHaven was formed as a community where we can do more than survive. Here, we can live and thrive, all seeking to take care of one another, and welcoming those who come to us from over the mountains.

"Here you have a chance to find your own way. None of you are indebted to us, but if you choose to stay, you will have the chance to be part of something greater. Here we are more than just a collection of persons. Here we are part of a whole."

As she speaks, I let her words wash over me. I cannot take my eyes away from the water just meters away. The sheer vastness of it overwhelms me.

11

My fingertips idle through the loose sand beneath me. Clarice continues, explaining the community meal times and options on where to take shelter. Some of the families could take to the houses further inland.

She finishes her words, leading a final welcoming applause to all of us new to the community. People greet each other with casual ease.

"What do you think?" A woman approaches from nearby. I had seen her in the marketplace earlier in one of the booths. It is hard to know how old she is, but not much older than me. Her blonde hair and tan skin make me wonder how long she has lived here by the beach.

"What?" I reply.

She laughs lightly. "I'm sorry," she says. "I forget what it's like. It always takes a little bit of time to get used to it. I'm sure."

"Get used to what?"

"Oh, all this." She gestures around. "Safety. Food. A number of people who care about each other."

"Yes." I turn my gaze to the water's edge, lapping in gentle waves against the smooth sand. "I suppose that's true."

"I'm Olivia." She extends her hand to me, which I take with a tentative grasp. "Why don't I show you around. Come on."

I follow her towards the marketplace, back to the booth where I had seen her before. Everywhere I look, I see ornate vases, brightly colored tapestries, blankets, yarns, pottery, leather goods. A variety of scents and colors.

"Go ahead," Olivia says. "Touch anything you like."

Tentatively, I reach out to the surface of a tapestry, an intricate woven piece. The blankets and other fabrics have a similar texture as well. "Where did all this come from?" I ask.

"One of the families keeps a little farm of alpacas just

outside the city."

"Alpacas?"

"They're like llamas."

"Llamas…"

She laughs once more, taking me aback just a bit. But when she speaks again, she sounds sincere. "Every time a new caravan arrives, I forget just how different all of this must seem to you compared to over there."

"Have you ever been?" I ask. "Over the mountain, I mean."

"No. I never have. I've always lived here, even before. I'm one of the people who helped create SeaHaven. But go and look around. There's plenty of time to learn all about that."

"Thanks. I think I will. It's nice to meet you, Olivia."

"It's nice to meet you too, Ash," she says.

I find my way down to the water, spying some of the children, barefooted, laughing, and kicking through the shallows, and I follow suit, sitting down to pull off my boots.

The water feels cool, pushing and pulling against my ankles. I gaze out towards the horizon, trying to find the edge before it gives way to the sky.

I cannot. What I see is shades of blue fading from the darkness of the water to pale blue sky, with nothing much more than a slight gradation in hue between them.

Down the way I spot Marcus standing alone in the sand, his childlike face a stark difference between his stoicism and the laughter coming from the other children. He watches them with a deadpan expression. He has not spoken a single word since we found him in the mountains.

"How you doing?" I ask as I approach.

He does not respond, except to glance briefly my way.

I crouch down next to him. "Did you get something to

eat?"

He nods, barely a glimmer of a smile crossing his eyes. It is clear to me that he is different from when we first met. I can't pinpoint why. That night in the forest, I had been sure he had been killed, whisked away by the zombies. Even now, the echo of his screams still haunts my memories. He turns to me with his vacant eyes.

"You've been through something. Haven't you?"

He nods. I place my hands on his shoulders and peer into his eyes.

"Listen to me, Marcus. You and me, we're safe now. Do you understand? I'm going to do everything in my power to make sure nothing like that ever happens to you again."

He smiles just slightly, a defiant light gleaming in his eyes.

"In fact, Marcus, I want you to listen. Do you hear it?"

He glances around, unsure what he is listening for.

"They're gone. I can't hear them anymore. Can you?"

A light passes over his expression, as he realizes their absence.

"The feeling of them is gone. Do you feel it too? We're free of them now, Marcus. We're free."

He throws his tiny arms around my neck. As I return the embrace, I finally succumb, allowing myself to believe these words as well.

We're free.

We're finally free.

Two

"You want to make this interesting?" Thorn asks, his gaze locked on the empty parking lot before us. We both crouch behind the wall on the roof of the building, crossbows at the ready. We'd been stalking a juvenile boar for the better part of the morning and hoped to take it back to the encampment.

"What?" I reply, hitching my weapon into position. "You mean stalking a wild pig through a vacant shopping center isn't interesting enough?"

He offers me a side grin, sliding his gaze over to me. "Let's say I get a hit in first."

I suppress my chuckle, but not enough.

"Hey, it could happen," he replies.

"Okay, go on."

"So, whichever one of us gets the first hit has to do the other's chores for a week."

"Chores?" I respond. "That's what you want to bet on?"

"Why? You got something better?"

I don't have a chance to answer. The sound of scuttling hooves echoes off the concrete walls of the buildings all around us.

We had staked out on the roof of the single-story strip mall, our crossbows balanced on the wall's edge waiting for a target. Burnt-out lettering left behind nothing more than a large, red "T" and a lowercase "e." Across the street hung fallen wires, and a broken, dead-eyed stoplight rested askew in the middle of the intersection.

We both snap our attention back to the hunt. Fifty feet away, the brown, snuffling face of the wild pig wanders out around the edge of the building, unaware of our presence. Next to me, I sense Thorn tensing his grip around the crossbow, readying his aim.

"Not yet," I whisper, but he makes no sign that he hears me.

Seconds later, the bolt races from the flight groove. The pig squeals, a sharp pitch of fright and fury. I cringe, even though I know there are no zombies for miles which could be drawn by the sound. He scurries out of sight, disappearing behind the buildings.

"He's been hit," I say. I quickly disengage my crossbow, swinging it behind me before leaping to my feet. "Come on. We can track it."

Thorn does the same with his crossbow and follows me down the fire escape running along the side of the building to the sidewalk below. We cross the parking lot and I quickly spot the splash of blood against the concrete.

Following the trail for about three blocks, we locate the poor creature with his foot stuck in a grate between the sidewalk and the street, struggling against the final panic of his life. Thorn's arrow protrudes from its shoulder.

It doesn't have much left, but I approach from behind, drawing my hunting knife from its sheath. I straddle the pig and slice the blade across his neck, hot blood spraying my arms and face. With one more struggling spasm, life fades from its eyes.

"You win," I say, turning to Thorn. "You got the first hit."

He shrugs. "Yeah, but I didn't kill him. It doesn't count."

"Seriously though," I reply. "You've gotten a lot better. You've learned a lot in the last few months."

"Maybe I've had a good teacher," he says, stepping forward to help me free the hoof from the grate.

After field dressing the pig, we load it onto the wagon, one of many stashed around the city for just such a purpose. It takes us a solid hour to get back to camp, but when we arrive, we are welcomed with cheers and handshakes.

"It will be nice to have something besides fish," Clarice says, helping us haul the carcass to the hoist.

"Hey!" the older man, Charlie, I believe, protests from his spot on the pier a few feet away, manning his fishing pole. "I don't hear you complaining when the larders are full."

Clarice laughs, her bright smile shining like the sun. "Yes Charlie, you are absolutely right. We are lucky to have you." She turned to the two of us, gesturing us toward the fire. "Come. Let the others tend to the boar. You two have earned the day off."

Thorn wanders to the ever-present fire crackling in the circle of stones just above the high tide line. I kick off my shoes and step toward the gently lapping waves, splashing the water up my arms and face.

My clothes feel stiff from the morning's activity, the pig's blood having already dried against my skin. I peel away the shirt and tee underneath, stripping down to my bra and wading forward until the water meets my waist. The cool saltwater feels good, washing away the sweat and crud from the day's events.

Charlie waves to me from his spot on the edge of the pier, his gray mustache bobbing up and down as he squints out at the ocean. Next to him sits a cooler, loaded up with his cache of caught fish.

A pair of the older children run over to collect them, carting them off to the wood-smokers up the beach. I smile and wave back.

Up on the beach I hear the sounds of the citizens emerging from their houses, following the excited voices of the children celebrating our victorious hunt. Being this early in the day, Clarice and the others will have the pig roasting on the spit and ready before nightfall.

I turn to head back toward the beach when I see a tiny glint of light, just on the horizon. Perhaps just a flash of sunlight on the water, but Charlie stands up, raising one hand to shade his eyes.

He sees it too, whatever it is. I keep an eye on him as I head back over to Clarice, shaking the remnants of saltwater from my clothes.

"You haven't changed your clothes?" she says, looking me over with amusement. "What could be so important?"

"I'm not sure actually. There's something out there."

Clarice raises her hand and peers out to the horizon. I watch her face, surprised to find her concerned expression light up with a smile. "Ah, they're here," she murmurs, taking a step towards the water.

"Who? Who's here?"

"The islanders." She returns to assist with the preparation.

Another jubilant cheer rises from those gathered as she brings their attention to the arriving guests.

"Who are the islanders?" I ask Olivia, who had joined us.

"The Sea Dwellers," she says. "They live on the ocean, nomads. They came from the islands, originally. Bring us coffee and dried fruits and such. We offer them medicines when we can. Stuff like that. A chance to rest their feet on solid ground. It's always a big deal when they arrive."

"Yes, I see that." I peer out toward the horizon, trying to make out shapes, still only seeing a sliver of light as the sun hits them. "They live on the sea?"

"Oh yes," she replies. "They found a way to survive and thrive in this crazy world. They follow the currents and the wind from the islands up the East Coast, collecting and trading as they go."

I shake my head in disbelief, one hand absently rubbing

the back of my neck. "There's no zombies on the ocean."

"Exactly," she grins. "It's genius really."

Alma and Rose emerge from the beach house in which they made camp, walking up the beach hand in hand. As the ships loom closer, the children make a game out of running in and out of the waves.

I smile at their mirth, once more revealing the vast difference in the lifestyle these children will have compared to my own. Their happiness brings a smile to my face.

"Are you still having those headaches?" Olivia asks. I don't even realize I'd been pressing my fingers against my scalp.

"It's nothing," I reply quickly, lowering my arms. "Probably just the sunlight."

"You know, I'm sure Clarice could find something for you in the infirmary…"

"I said it's nothing!"

Her expression darkens for a moment, but she quickly gives a stiff smile. I immediately regret snapping at her, but already she joins the others in their merriment around the firepit.

Over the course of the day, the ships veer closer to the coast, moving as one unit. Once close enough, I can make out the structure of their flotilla. A series of small wooden boats loosely bound together by a series of ropes, enough give between them for steering.

One person sits in each vessel, men and women with considerable strength in their arms and shoulders, no doubt, from the practice of rowing. While the boats are small, the collective creates a considerable blot against the sea.

As they draw nearer, I realize larger ships and houseboats make up the far side of the fleet. All together their structure appears like a huge floating island, each vessel making up a part of a larger structure.

The complexity of the combined structures takes my breath away, reminding me in some ways of the buildings in the center of the city.Windows and balconies along the outer houseboats have persons peering back at us, waving and smiling to those of us on the shore.

They make their way to shore on small row boats carrying no more than thirty or forty people. Not one of them looked like me, either. They all had beautiful dark skin like Clarice and Simeon, carrying the same bright smiles as well.

By the time evening rolls around, the majority of the newcomers have made their way ashore. The crackling scent of the roasted pig wafts over the beach, beckoning the remaining citizens.

Clarice takes the initiative, serving out generous portions of food. Potatoes, carrots, and zucchini, grown in the inland plots, nestle in the coals until brought to a steaming crisp, topped with sizzling, shredded pork.

Once the younger children go off to bed, and the laughter dies down, one of the elder women regales us with stories of her homeland, describing how they created their floating community after the islands had been overtaken by the zombies.

She takes her seat by the fire, and the flickering light glows against her white hair and brown skin as she tells us the story of their history. Silence falls over those of us listening, taking in the seriousness of her words, the pain reflected in her eyes as she recalls the days before the Fall.

"When we die," she says, nearing the end, "there will exist a world in which no one remembers how it was before. A world in which you have grown up knowing only this, how to survive day by day. But perhaps therein lies the hope." She turns her gaze towards us, Thorn, Alma, Rose, and I, sitting among the others near our age, Olivia, Sarah, and the rest.

"Perhaps you can succeed where we have failed," she continues. "Create a new world where such a tragedy would never happen again. A world in which you can not only survive, but thrive, as you are intended to do." She raises her hands, facing her palms towards us. "May Papa Legba open the doors and the loa guide your footsteps as you walk."

This final declaration seems to break the spell. She stands, brushing her hands against her legs. Chats and good nights float through the crowd. Sleep tempts behind my eyes and the excitement of the day catches up to me. My mind drifts through her story as I wander back to the house where I had my camp.

I can't imagine a world different than this. Constantly watching around every corner, aware of every sound, every step, every movement. But the presence of SeaHaven proves that people can live without fear.

And now, having learned about these people, who have made for themselves a whole community on the water, living free of zombies, could such a thing be possible, I wonder, on a grander scale?

It is too much to think on. I make my way back to my room, one of many in the large, abandoned house. I spot Rose and Alma outside the door of Alma's room, standing close to each other, talking quietly. They don't see me approach at first.

Their intimate talking segues into a kiss in such a way that I have seen others kiss, Clarice and Simeon, and some of the other young couples.

I stay to the shadows, slowing my movement. They embrace, slow and lingering, arms around each other. It had never occurred to me that two women could kiss like that. I step back, kicking my feet a bit to alert them of my presence. They break apart from each other and smile my way, Alma's arm draping casually over Rose's shoulders.

"Everything alright?" Alma says, arching an eyebrow.

"Of course," I say with a smirk. "Carry on. Don't mean to interrupt."

Inside my room, I find Marcus curled up on the animal skins laid out for our bedding, his soft breath steady in the depths of sleep. The shadow of his lashes flicker against his pink cheek.

I kick off my shoes and take my place perpendicular from him, pulling the skins around my shoulders. My mind calms in the silence of the room, the darkness and moonlight streaming through the window, leaving a puddle of silver on the floor of the otherwise empty room.

Three

When I wake, at least a few hours have passed. It is now fully dark, but the angle of the moonlight casts against the wall. I hear distant hoofbeats against pavement, moving at a steady trot, triggering adrenaline. Immediately, I sit up, moving away from Marcus carefully. The horse is blocks away still, and for a brief moment, I am grateful for my elevated senses.

Someone is coming.

As slow as I can, I reach for my crossbow, moving at a crawl until I get past the door frame. I stand up, moving the weapon against my back and keeping my arm at an angle to grab it quickly if I need it.

Barefoot, I run up the beach away from the camps until I arrive at the wooden planks of the docks. I circle around to the east side of the houses, nearing the street where the sound is coming from, inland. I make my way down the stairs, tucking into the shadows underneath and watching the length of the moonlit streets.

The horse appears, slowed to a walk, head down, ears forward. At first, I think I am seeing brown winter fur, but as it moves closer, I realize it is mud and dirt caked on the creature's flanks and tangled mane.

The rider also has his head down. I cannot see his face. He might be injured. In the dim light, I cannot quite make out what I am seeing.

With one swift movement, I swing around the crossbow, positioning the cross hairs on the rider, just in case.

The horse steps into a patch of moonlight. With a rush of recognition, I place the crossbow on the ground and step out into the light, hands raised at shoulder level. The rider holds steady, but fatigue shows on his face. I know this face all too well.

"Ash, is that you?" A long-ago, familiar voice comes from the figure on the horse.

"Yes, Ezekiel. It's me."

"Oh, thank God," he mutters, pitching forward. I catch him, just as he loses purchase on the horse, tumbling into my arms. The moment his feet touch the ground, his knees buckle.

"Ash. You have to come back. She's figured out how to control them.

"It's okay," I say, steadying him. "I've got you. I've got you, Ezekiel."

"The horse," he mumbles.

"We'll water her. She'll be alright."

With one arm around him, and the other holding the horse's bridle, we head back towards the encampment. I take him to the fire pit, still smoldering from the day's activities.

We pass by some tents, and I call out to wake the others. Rose appears, still in her tee shirt and boxers, her usual sleeping clothes. She immediately starts stoking the fire to get it going again. Alma meets me on the other side of Ezekiel, supporting his other arm and helping him sit down by the fire. Simeon rushes from his tent, carrying with him the water skein for the new guest.

"I know him," I say to the gathered few. "This is Eden's son, Ezekiel."

"I'll tend to the horse," Clarice says, approaching us from the same tent she shares with Simeon.

"Yes, but come back quickly," Eva says. "We may need your help."

"Yes, of course," Clarice says, picking up on her meaning. She and Simeon exchange a glance, before she pulls on her boots and slips away.

Simeon tips the water flask to Ezekiel's lips and he drinks.

When Clarice returns, she carries with her a vial of oil, tilting his head back and placing a few drops on his tongue.

Together she and Simeon carry him to the infirmary, such as it was. Whatever he had to say to us could wait until morning.

"It can't be good," Eva says. "Him being here. What do you think it means?"

"I don't know. But you're right. It can't be good."

Not until well into the following day did I receive word that he asked for me. One of Clarice's girls came to fetch me at the water's edge.

I had not slept since his arrival. This had been the longest night since arriving at SeaHaven. We walk in silence up the grassy hillside toward the infirmary, one of the few buildings which has not been taken by the overgrown flora.

Ezekial sits up, sipping at a plastic cup of water. The room appears plain, a bed in one corner and a side table containing a pitcher, which had been filled from the water stores.

Olivia had placed some bright purple flowers in a vase at the window. These details I have yet to get used to in this new way of life. Pieces of beauty such as this are a luxury that bare survival does not allow.

Ezekiel's eyes widen when he sees me. "You're alive," he says.

"Of course I'm alive," I mutter.

"Well, thank god I found you."

He looks like he's been through hell. A greasy sheen permeates his hair, dirty brown from the layer of dust. He would need a bath sometime soon.

"Are you infected?" I ask.

"Ash!" Olivia chided.

"What?" I reply. "No point in beating around the bush.

Either he is, or he isn't."

"I'm not," Ezekiel replied. "It's a fair question."

"Okay, then. You have my audience. What's going on Ezekiel? What brought you here?"

"Ash, we need your help."

"What's going on?" I ask, settling in at the edge of the bed.

"We need help," he says, his voice tinged in desperation.

"There's not enough of us left. She's taken too many of us." His gaze darts around the room, as if searching. For what, I can't know.

"Wait, wait. Slow down. We have time, Ezekiel. Start from the beginning."

He takes a deep, shuddering breath. "Yes. Yes, let's do that." He glances around, taking in Olivia and Simeon, and then back to me. I can see the torture behind his eyes.

"What happened after we left?"

"After you left, I decided to leave the farm. I wanted to try and find my way on my own. Mom and Dad weren't thrilled about the idea, but they couldn't stop me. Dad said I was old enough, and I knew how to survive the land. I promised them I would go into the mountains."

"The mountains." A sense of dread bloomed in my stomach, recalling the scoundrels who had accosted us, the ones who had Marcus.

"For a couple of weeks, I camped. I had my bug-out bag, and I had literally trained my whole life for over-ground survival. I did alright. I really did. I got as high as I could, hiking up the mountain, just moving forward. I didn't know how many days I'd been hiking when I stopped seeing them. By the time I realized it, I hadn't seen a zombie for at least three days.

"I set up camp then. A real camp where I could stay for a

bit. Before that, I'd been sleeping in trees. Trying to keep moving."

"How does that work?" Olivia asks. "Sleeping in trees..."

He rolled his eyes towards her, cocking a half-smile. "I tied myself in my sleeping bag to the largest tree branch. Trust me. After that, I never knew the cold hard ground could feel so comfortable."

"I know that feeling," I said.

"So, I camped out for a few weeks without much trouble. Spent my time hunting, mostly. Foraging, filtering water. That kind of stuff. I guess I was just trying to figure out my next move. And then one day, I woke up and discovered I wasn't alone."

"Zombies?" I ask.

"No." He gives me a half-grin. "Them."

"*Them*? What the hell does that mean?"

"The scavengers. The ones who live in the mountains," Ezekiel continued. "Seems you may have had a run in with them on the way over?"

I recall the moment we found out we were not alone. The woman dressed in white who held our lookout at knife point. The stand-off between the two of us. I had been the one who spotted Marcus in their midst. For whatever reason, I believe it was the crossbow I had leveled at her head, she returned Marcus to us. She had called me Baby A. I never got her name.

"I remember."

Ezekiel continued, "I woke up to find them surrounding my camp, weapons drawn. The woman was the only one unarmed. She looked... I don't know how to describe her."

"Clean," I said. "She looked clean."

"Yes, oddly so. I've never seen anyone outside of the farm that clean, especially wearing all white the way she did. She approached me. Hell, I was barely dressed. I'd only managed to pull on my jeans before stepping out of the tent.

"But she asked me my name, and when I told her, she gestured for everyone to lower their weapons. All of this was just for effect, I'll bet. Nearly everything she does looks like a production."

"To let you know she's in charge."

"Exactly." He glanced out the window. "But once I got in with them, spent some time with them, I learned there were far less than they used to be. They took me in, fed me, the whole deal. But once I figured out what had been happening, I knew I had to find you."

"What's been happening then?" I ask.

"People are being taken." He stops, his eyes reflecting some witnessed horror. "I don't know how, but she's controlling them. The doctor."

"Tell me," I whisper, trying my best to keep my voice steady.

"The current theory is, she's trying to recreate whatever happened when they made you."

I wince at his words, but he is not wrong. The implications make my stomach turn.

"People have been disappearing for weeks now, always girls. Always teenagers and young women. Like you, Ash."

"How do you know this is her doing?" I ask.

"At first we didn't. We thought a few of them might have run off or something like that. But it kept happening. Always at night.

"The first one gone was Jessa Turner. She's always been a bit of a rebel. Fairlight thought she'd run away. Jessa's mother was upset of course. We all felt bad, but no one really took it serious until Angela went missing. Then Sadie, then Beth. We've had about one disappearance a week.

"How long has it been since the first girl went missing?"

"That would have been about two months ago," he says, counting out the time on his fingertips. "Now it's not just the girls though. It's everyone. They've taken all the children older than ten, and nearly half of the adults. We've lost nearly three-fourths of the tribe. And we can't get away from them, no matter how far we go. Those creatures have figured out how to climb the mountains."

"They're being taken by zombies?" Olivia asks. "Have you seen it?"

Ezekiel nods, lifting his face towards me, anguished eyes locked on mine. "Yes. They got past our night watch. We set up camp to circle our most vulnerable, but they still got through."

"How can that be?" I say.

"I don't know, but I saw them. They move with purpose. They're fast, too. They're not like the mindless beings we're familiar with. This is a whole new monster. They're horrifying to look at because they move as if they have thought." He gazes out the window towards the west. He continues, "It's only a matter of time before they cross the mountains. You're not safe here. You're not safe anywhere, anymore."

I look at him, incredulous. "You can't be serious."

He nods. "Will you help us?"

Ezekiel and I have our differences. Even now, part of me thinks it's not fair for him to ask me. I've gotten away. That part of my life is over. Or at least it was. But even so, seeing the desperation etched on his face, the horror in his words... How can I turn my back on them now? I turn to the others standing at the edge of the room.

"Could you guys give us a minute?" I ask.

I don't respond until Ezekiel and I are the only two left in the small room. "I'll come with you," I say. "But it's not going to

29

be what you want me to do. I can help you relocate, find a safe space. Maybe we can bring them here to settle in SeaHaven…"

"She'll never go for it."

"It might be your only option. At least for a little while. Besides, if she's controlling them somehow, there's really only one thing I can do."

"What's that?"

"I'm going to find her. I'll find Doctor Donovan and confront her."

"Confront her? You have to fight the zombies, Ash. You're the only one who has the ability to overpower them, to stop them. I don't see how having a chat with Doctor Donovan will help anything."

"She has to see what she is doing is wrong, Ezekiel. I could fight them, but then what? They'll just keep coming. They outnumber us. I can't stop all of them. I have to go to the source, which happens to be her."

"And what if she doesn't? Then what are you going to do?"

"I'm going to give her a chance. One chance. Then, I'm going to burn that place to the ground. That's what I'm going to do."

Four

Leaving the infirmary, I head back to the fire. There, I find Thorn stoking it with a stick to get the blaze going again. In the eastern horizon, a thin orange line heralds the morning sun.

"There's salmon in the smokehouse if you're hungry," Thorn says. "But the coffee is hot."

"I'll eat later. But I will have coffee." I sit down, lifting the boiler kettle from the side of the coals. Grabbing one of the tin mugs, I pour myself a cup of coffee.

"What did he say?" Thorn asks, keeping his gaze on the fire.

"He's asking me to come back. They need my help."

"So do you think you'll go?" I know it is not really a question.

"I have to," I say.

"Why do you have to?"

"You know why, Thorn. I can't let her keep doing these things. Someone has to stop her."

"Why does that someone have to be you?"

"Who else would it be?" I reply.

"What if you didn't go?" Thorn says.

"Just what are you getting at, Thorn?" I say with some annoyance.

He focused his eyes on the fire, flames flickering, casting shadows against his face. "Just… that you're here now. It's safe here."

I keep to myself the details of what Ezekiel had told me. I haven't yet decided how much I want to tell him about the sentient zombies.

Sentient. How ironic.

31

"You were safe in the compound," I say. "But you were ready to leave there because it was the right thing to do. How is this different?"

"None of us were safe in the compound!" he snaps.

"Exactly," I reply. "And who was in charge there? Dr. Donovan. She's dangerous. She needs to be stopped."

He shakes his head, brushing the errant hair off of his forehead. "She's not dangerous to *you* though, Ash. She's there. You're here."

I rub my hand against my cheeks. "Look. I didn't want to tell you all of this. Ezekiel says she's controlling them somehow. She's making them kidnap members of the tribe."

"What's she doing with them?" Thorn asks.

"I don't know. I really don't, but I can guarantee it's not good. He says she's controlling them somehow. The zombies are stronger. They can go farther and move faster. And it's only a matter of time before they figure out a way over the mountains."

He tosses the stick into the fire, now leaping with hot orange flames against the background of the ocean sunrise. "Then we go somewhere else," he says. "We go farther south. Maybe we hitch a ride to the flotilla when they go. I don't know. Something."

"Thorn, I get it. Really, I do. But if we're not safe here, we're not safe anywhere. And we have to think about everyone. Clarice, Simeon. Rose. What about them? If we want to rebuild, we have to make it a clean start. And that won't happen unless someone stops Donovan. Otherwise, we'll just be running for the rest of our lives."

He stares hard into the fire, sipping at his coffee. "I know you're right," he murmurs. "I just don't like it."

"Neither do I."

"I'm coming with you."

"What? No," I reply.

"Why not?" He glances at me, the morning sun shadowed by the fringe of hair across forehead.

"Look, I'll talk with Simeon and Clarice. We'll decide who is best to go with me. But I'm not taking anyone with me who hasn't grown up out there. You and Rose grew up in the compound, behind thick walls which kept you safe. At least from them."

He glares at me with burning eyes.

"I don't mean-- Look, it's not that you can't take care of yourself. But when you have to defend against them, over time you develop kind of a second nature about them."

"I'm sure some more than others," he mutters.

"What's that supposed to mean?"

"No, Ash… I didn't mean… Look, you don't have to go and save the world all the time. I mean…" His expression softens.

"I like the way you are here."

His words surprise me. My desire to not get into an argument wins out. "Yeah?"

"Yeah. I mean, sometimes you smile since we've arrived. I like seeing that."

"Is that so?" I chide him by twisting my face into a clownish grin. "I'm sorry if my face was too busy killing zombies to stop and smile all the time."

"Ash, stop it. You know what I mean."

"What do you mean?" I bare my teeth and bug my eyes at him.

"I mean," he snaps, "I like seeing you happy!"

I fall silent and we watch the sunrise, a fiery medallion rising over the rough-surfaced sea.

"Who do you think you'll take with you?" he asks after a long while.

"I'm not sure yet. Ezekiel is taking me as far as the tribe, so he'll be leaving with me at least."

"You know, he didn't grow up with them either."
I shoot Thorn a side glance. "I'm pretty sure Ezekiel was training for the zombie apocalypse long before anybody knew we would have one."

Thorn nods with a light chuckle. "You may have a point there."

I reach down and pick up a handful of sand, letting it flow through my fingers. "I thought Alma, for sure. She's strong. She would be a real asset out there. There's a few of the others. I might talk to Simeon about who has experience with them."

"What about Rose?"

"Rose is out. She's the same as you. I need to teach the two of you how to deal with them. I mean, really deal with them. No offense, but you're both too soft to be of any use out there."

"Oh, I'm soft, am I?" He grins and pinches me lightly on the shoulder.

"Yeah, you are," I reply, returning the pinch, but a little bit harder.

"Hey, ow!" He tackles me, throwing us both off the stump and tumbling onto the sand. Almost on instinct, I shift my body weight to toss him over onto his back, my legs straddling his hips and feet hooked around his legs to pin him in place.

"Gotcha," I say evenly. "You can't even fight off a girl. What makes you think you're any match for a zombie." He laughs, and I have to admit the way his eyes glow in the rising sun makes me want to…

"I was holding back," he says. "I didn't want to hurt you," he replies with a slow grin.

"Oh, I'm sure. So, if this happened…" I dig the toe of my boot into his leg, "you'd be able to defend yourself?"

"Of course!" He gritted his teeth against the pressure.

"What about this?" I pin his wrists down and lean forward. Gently, I nip at his face, catching the flesh of his cheek between my teeth but applying very little pressure. I finish the move with a little zombie growl.

"Oh, I've been bit!" he calls, flailing about enough to throw my hands off. The shift of balance tips me over. I roll over onto my back, and he leans up next to me, our faces now inches from each other. The mood turns suddenly quiet.

The sunlight catches through the edges of his amber eyes, turning them into fire. I feel the heat rising to my cheeks, despite myself.

"See?" he murmurs softly, brushing a stray lock of hair from my forehead, the tips of his fingers tracing lightly against my cheek. "When you're here, you get to be normal."

His words hit me like a punch in the stomach. Now my cheeks burn for a different reason. I push him away and scramble backwards to my feet, turning away so he can't see my face.

"Ash," he calls after me. "Ash, wait." I hear the immediate regret in his voice, but I don't care.

"I gotta go, Thorn," I blurt out over my shoulder, scrambling to get away from him. "Some of us have a long hike in front of us."

He keeps calling out to me as I distance myself, but he doesn't follow.

Good. I don't want him to.

Ezekiel sleeps through most of the day, finally emerging from the infirmary just as the citizens gathered for the evening meal. He joins us, taking great pleasure in the food set out before us, the leftover wild boar, fresh crisp apples, and loaves of the hearty, earthen bread which Olivia was so fond of making. He bathed in the ocean after his meal, an exercise in refreshment more than cleanliness.

As evening approaches, we congregate by the fire. Myself, Clarice and Simeon, Alma, Rose, Thorn, and Ezekiel.

"We should leave at first light," Ezekiel says, glancing towards the west. "We'll need the daylight to cover more ground. If we go early, we can make it to the camp within the day."

Thorn keeps looking at me. We had not spoken since morning. I drag my boot through the sand, leaving a trench the width of my heel, but I don't return his gaze.

"What is it they want?" Clarice asks, speaking in her clear, clipped accent, making no pretense to hide her concern. "How is this something you cannot solve? Why do you need our Ash?" Ezekiel's eyes flick towards me.

"It's okay," I say. "They know."

"She can help us," he explains. "Ash has the ability to stop these creatures, possibly even stop them for good. If that doesn't happen soon, we could all be in danger." He repeats to them the unfortunate events happening in the mountains, the missing children, the desperation of the tribe.

"I don't like it," Clarice says, shaking her head. "These are the same people who held you hostage on your journey back." She turns to Simeon. "How do we know they can be trusted?"

"We have a common foe," he replies softly. "We must help them if we can."

"Excuse me," I interrupt their quiet conversation. "I don't think it's up to either one of you."

Everyone turns to look at me. Alma holds a gleam in her eye, one which I recognize. Out of everyone present, she is the only one I trust fully to be able to survive out there. I meet her gaze, and she gives me a slight nod.

"Of course, I'll go," I say. "The good doctor and I have

some unfinished business. I thought it had been taken care of before I came here, but obviously I was wrong."

"I'll come," Alma says, returning my gaze with her steely eyes. Rose looks at her with a wide, worried expression.

"You're under no obligation," I say. "I know you have made a place here."

"Yes. And that's all the more reason. Besides, I haven't forgiven her for what happened to Travis."

She turns to Rose, sitting next to her with their fingers laced.

"Go," Rose says quietly. "I'll be here when you get back."

I turn to Ezekiel. "I'm assuming you are well enough to show us the way to the encampment?"

"Of course," he replies with a wry smile.

"Good, then we leave at first light."

I don't much care for the idea of heading back over the mountains by foot. Ezekiel says he knows about a pass through the ridge which would shorten our trip by half a day.

He promised he could lead us to the encampment where Fairlight and the rest stayed. We gather at the firepit before the sun comes up, myself, Ezekiel, and Alma.

We wait for the others to come and see us off. Clarice wanted to give us each an amulet for luck. Rose came along with Alma, her face etched with sadness.

I drag my heel through the sand, my thick boot leaving a foot-sized trench.

"We'd better get on the road," I say. "We need the daylight."

"Yeah. The encampment is about a day's hike from here. If we leave within the next hour, we'll get there before dark."

"Are they on this side?" I ask. "Fairlight's camp, I mean? This side of the ridge."

"For now. They're being careful to make sure they're not being followed. They didn't want to risk the only help available."

"Fair enough," I say, but I stop listening. As the others ready their packs and prepare for the journey, I glance over to Thorn, lingering at the water's edge a few meters away.

He glances up as I approach, but I look away. I have my eye on the water's edge. As we are about to embark on a long hike inland, I kick off my shoes and step out into the lapping wavelets. It feels good, and I won't be feeling it for a while. I did not want to leave things between me and Thorn the way we did, but I don't know what to say.

We leave no more than an hour later, the three of us loaded up with goods. I have my crossbow strapped across my back, various pouches of food in my pack. Alma carries a similar setup, with the addition of a couple of blades tucked into her waist. Ezekiel has a shotgun strapped to his back, with strict orders from Simeon not to use it unless absolutely necessary.

"The noise will attract them," he said. "But we're dealing with something we don't know about, so I want you to have it, just in case."

I had not felt the pull since arriving here in SeaHaven. I don't look forward to being around them again, even within a few miles I can feel them. I don't like the part of me which wakes up when they're around me.

At least I have the ability to avoid them and fight them off when I need to. Maybe things would have gone differently if I'd been there. Abraham and Eden might have had a chance, but I wasn't there.

We walk in silence, stopping now and then for water and chatting now and then, about nothing much. Ezekiel keeps quiet most of the time, his famous scowl parked firmly on his face.

"So what's going on with you and Rose?" I ask Alma

during one particularly dry stretch. Ezekiel had proceeded ahead by a few feet, so we had some relative privacy.

"I don't know," Alma says. "I could ask you the same thing about you and Thorn."

"Hardly." I took the invitation to drop the subject. She had lost Travis just before we left for the mountains from Eden's farm. He had been infected during the raid on the compound. I suspected it was when he plowed his truck through the horde of zombies with his driver's side window down.

She took it well when it happened, staying by his side for days as he slowly deteriorated. In the end, she was the one who took him down.

When we round the path into a clearing, I hear a crack of a branch from within the tree line up ahead. Ezekiel holds up a fist to signal us to stop.

I suppress the urge to point out his folly. If we hear their movements, they have already been watching us for some time. If we hear a branch breaking, it's because they want us to hear it.

The three of us step into the middle of the clearing. I keep my arms slightly elevated, palms forward. The weight of my crossbow gives me some comfort.

Following my cue, Ezekiel and Alma do the same, keeping a small distance between us. I watch the shadows, searching for movement. They appear slowly, molding out of the shadows, each of them carrying a bladed weapon, knives, axes.

They step forward until we are surrounded by about thirty of them, still completely silent. They had gotten good at this.

Just in front of me, she appears. Again, she stands with confidence, even though she is the only one without a weapon in hand. Though I do notice the large Bowie knife strapped to her hip in the white leather holster.

Her pristine white pants and crisp white tee shirt accent

the petiteness of her frame. She keeps her hands to her side except to gesture for the others to lower their weapons. I step forward, keeping my eyes steady on her.

"Hello Fairlight," I say.

"Ash Donovan," she says with a purposeful grin. "We meet again."

Five

"There's no reason for all these theatrics, y'all," she calls to the people around her, speaking in her signature southern accent. "She is an invited guest, after all. Come on, let's get y'all back to camp. I bet you're ready for somethin' to eat."

Alma nods. "I could eat."

We walk for another two miles or so into a complex maze of chasms, traveling in silence. It quickly becomes clear they chose this area because of the difficulty of the terrain, to keep hidden what remained of their tribe. Briefly, we stop at a creek's edge to refill our canteens.

"We must be getting close," I say. "I smell roasting meat."

"That would be us. Camp is about a quarter mile down the creek a ways. Thought we'd break out the finery since we're embarking on a truce and all."

"Well, I'm starving," Alma says. She takes a swig of her water.

"Yep," Ezekiel says. "We're not far now."

Just under ten minutes later, we round the corner to the camp. We had followed the stream into the natural enclosure of the box canyon.

The water flows into an underground tunnel, and the area is surrounded on three sides by towering stone walls smoothed over by time and erosion. Here and there, the rocks are dotted with fauna.

Up ahead, a large bonfire blazed, sending a plume of smoke up the center of the canyon. I noticed the depth of the camp was such that the smoke dissipated enough by the time it reached the top, keeping the camp well-hidden from both humans and non-humans alike.

However, the succulent wild turkey roasting in the edge of the flames did little to divert any wild animals that might be in the area. My mouth waters at the tempting aroma.

"Since we found this place, we've fared well," Fairlight said, as she steps alongside of me. "Do you see the armed lookouts at the tops there?"

I peer upwards to the top of the canyon, where she gestures on both sides. "I don't see anyone."

"Exactly." She smirks. "Y'all can wash up in the stream there, but be careful of the current. It gets stronger closer to the canyon wall."

"Of course," I reply.

"Make yourself at home. We'll eat shortly."

I glance around, silently counting the number of people left in the camp, doing a mental comparison to the larger group we saw last year.

No more than twelve, a scraggle of people. Each of them carrying a weight of sadness in their eyes and shoulders. I cannot imagine the loss they must have experienced. Now and then, someone catches my gaze, glancing away quickly with an unmistakable excitement, a spark of hope flickering against the darkness of the palpable sadness.

I make my way to the water's edge, taking a moment to splash the cool liquid onto my arms and face to refresh from the day's hike. It feels good and cold against my skin, and I lower the lip of my canteen to fill it up. Deciding that the ground here looks even enough, mostly rock, some grass and pebbles, I pull off my shoes and dip my sore feet into the running water.

Alma approaches and sits down next to me. "Good idea," she says, as she lowers her bare feet into the water. "Aah! That feels so good and cold!" She lay back against the grassy shore.

As I splash the water over my forearms, I take a moment

to examine the gaping hole leading to the underground cave. I do not particularly prefer to be this close to it, but I want to get a good look before moving away. Though the diameter is not more than three feet, there is enough space for someone to crawl through as long as they did not care to get wet. I cannot help but imagine the darkness permeating the depths of the underground caverns.

"Food's on!" one of the others calls from close to the fire.

"Oh, blessed be! I'm starving," Alma mutters.

The food is parceled out by one of the members cutting up the meat, having transferred the steaming bird to the clean tree stump to carve it into manageable slices. These are then wrapped into an edible leaf, dandelion by the looks of it, to guard our fingertips against the heat. Portions are passed around to everyone. I wait for the others to begin before I tuck into mine. As much as I hate to wait, I figure it is only polite.

The three of us, Alma, Ezekiel, and I, sit cross-legged next to Fairlight. She quickly finishes her small portion before standing to address those gathered.

"For those of you who don't know yet," she began to speak in her quiet, yet fierce, voice, "we have some guests with us I'd like to introduce to everyone. You already know Ezekiel of course. He's managed to find the one he's told us about. She and her companion have come to help us. This is Alma, and this," she gestures towards me, "is Ash Donovan. The one they called Baby A. Ash, would you like to say a few words?"

"Are you all the one's who will bring our people back?" a woman speaks from the gathering shadows. I seek her out, finding a disheveled woman with dirty blonde hair practically clinging to the man next to her, equally disheveled. I realize her question prompted all eyes towards me, including Fairlight. To my surprise, even she held a flicker of a question in her eyes.

I stand up to be able to address them better. "I, um…" Being on the spot like this, I struggle with what to say. They all peer at me with these wide, desperate eyes, the losses of their family members hanging palpable in the air. "I don't know what I can do to bring them back," I say. "But I'll do everything I can to stop what's been happening. Perhaps it would help me if some of you could tell me a little bit about it."

"Our daughter," the woman said. "She was the one most recently taken, before we found this canyon. It hasn't happened since we found this place."

The man next to her turns away, his jaw muscles working to suppress his emotions. The woman fumbled with a locket around her neck, flipping it open and handing it forward to me. The picture inside is hand-drawn but quite clear. The image depicts a little blonde girl with a unique, crooked smile.

Fairlight approaches, placing her hand on my arm. "The last few months have been hard on all of us," she says, speaking to everyone. "Baby A is special. She has promised to help as well as she can."

"Ash," I say.

"What?"

"You keep calling me Baby A. My name is Ash."

"Of course," she says with deference. "Ash."

"What does it mean anyway? Baby A."

"It means you were the first."

Ezekiel leans in toward me, just slightly. "Does that mean there are others like you? Is there a Baby B and so on?"

I don't answer right away, but my mind flickers back to the conversation between me and Marcus that night in the forest. How close I came to losing him. I return to my seat, picking up my food again, forcing myself to eat.

At least, at the very least, we make it through the majority of our meal before it happens. At first, I don't even realize… but there is a sound, just a whisper of a growl, emanating from deep within the ground. I feel certain no one else can hear it. Just me and my heightened senses, what Fairlight considers "special."

"What's wrong?" Alma asks, peering intently at my face.

"I don't know. Something is close by. The tunnel."

She turns her gaze to the opening where the stream flows into the wall. "It can't be," she whispers, shaking her head ever so slightly.

"What is it?" Fairlight approaches, seeing the exchange between us. I extend my mental reach, trying to see if I can connect with whatever it is under the ground. It's one of them for sure, but there is something different about the feeling of it.

Considering these are sentient enough to kidnap a child, either they still have some shred of active mental capacity or Dr. Donovan has cracked the code in controlling them.

"Get everyone north," I say. "Out of the canyon if possible."

"But--"

"Now!" The headache hits me, like a spike through my temple, about three seconds before the zombie erupts out of the tunnel.

Fairlight speaks in a calm but serious tone, speaking over the screams, and directing the panicked crowd away from the threat. "Just move normally, but quickly. Head for the grove of trees at the canyon's edge."

The headache puts me under. I feel useless, utterly useless. I plant the ball of my hand against my forehead, wincing at the sudden pain.

The sun had already dipped well below the high walls of the canyon, but even the remaining twilight felt like a dagger through my eyes. I collapse forward onto all fours and vomit onto the ground before everything goes black.

When I come to, the pain has stopped. Ezekiel had killed the zombie, and the two of them had pulled it from the tunnel. The pain, though gone, had left behind a strange euphoria. I felt as if I could barely move.

"Let me see it," I say.

"You need to lie down," Alma says. "You don't need to be looking at anything right now."

"I want to see it." I pull myself up to sitting.

"Let her see it," Ezekiel says, returning to our location. He and I exchange a glance. For the most part, the two of us have nothing short of animosity for each other, but in that brief moment, I feel an inkling of respect for him. Very few people could handle the presence of an actual zombie.

He holds his hand out to me, pulling me to my feet. I feel badly for tarnishing their camp, but already some of the women are wringing a cloth over the sick I had left.

The creature appears rather water-logged, exposed arms covered in swollen yellowish skin, peeling and split with black ooze seeping from within. This one had been underground for a good while.

"Pull the knife out," I say.

"Ash."

"Bring it out here. I want to see it."

He hesitates, but watches my expression for several seconds. He motions toward one of the camp members and together they each took an arm, leveraging the creature out of the tunnel. Fairlight approaches, carefully observing the three of us.

"Has this happened before?" I say.

"Not here," she replies.

"Do you think this is one of the fast ones?"

"Without a doubt. You may not have seen it, but it was

pushing itself through the tunnel, climbing out with intentional movements, pushing against the side of the walls."

The zombie looked like he used to be a regular person. He wore a tee shirt and jeans, mainly rotted away from the exposure to the underground alkaline water. The ground sways just a bit and Fairlight takes my arm.

"Maybe I do need to lie down," I say.

She leads me to a small inlet within the stone wall of the canyon where they had laid out makeshift beds for us, a leather pallet laid over a parcel of clean hay spread on the ground. She tucks me in, pulling the tanned animal hide over me.

All I want is to lie still and close my eyes, but I spot Alma a few feet away, dampening a cloth with a plastic bottle of water. She glances my way with a crease of worry around her eyes. I wave her over.

"You okay?" she says.

"I will be. I just need to close my eyes for a bit." She does not appear convinced, but she places the cool cloth on my forehead. "I'm sorry I lost it back there," I say.

"Yeah, what happened there? Did that thing get in your head?"

"I'm not exactly sure. I mean, you've seen me around them before. You saw how it was at Eden's farm when we went up to clear the fence?"

"Yeah, I remember."

"It's always been unpleasant, but nothing like this."

She adjusts the cloth, pulling it down over my eyes. "Try and get some rest," she says. "We'll need you alert when the time comes. They're fortifying the entrance, but I heard them say something about moving camp tomorrow."

"Probably not a bad idea," I mumble, feeling the pull of sleep already overtaking my body.

"I'll be over there if you need anything. Just give me a shout, okay?"

"Okay, I will." By the time she steps away, the post-migraine euphoria has kicked into overdrive. I know the others are staying up to talk, but within seconds I can no longer hear them.

Six

The following week remains largely uneventful, which allows me to gain a layout of the landscape. The mornings consist of venturing out to explore.

Most of the time I go alone, but on occasion I like to trail along with the hunting group. The first three days after the incident we spent relocating camp to another area within the canyons. This one held a small trickle of water coursing down from the rocks. It did not appear as secure as the box canyon, but at least we had one curved wall as a source of protection.

We set up a scheduled watch on the remaining three sides of the camp. This gave me plenty of time to take up my crossbow once more. Even during my time at SeaHaven, I did not let myself grow lax in my discipline. I never know when I'll need it. But other than the incident with the zombie from under the mountain,

I don't see any more of them.

But I feel them.

They are here, somewhere just out of sight. Around the bend, over the horizon. That sensation of my skin crawling, of something scratching inside me to get out, I had almost forgotten what it felt like.

Ezekiel shows me the best hunting areas. With me along, he decides to leave his shotgun behind on most days. He prefers knives, I think, because of the potential for close combat. He likes the risk. Also, they are quite useful for skinning badgers, and sometimes, if we get really lucky, a deer.

Through this time, we forged a bit of a tentative friendship. I see in his eyes he still does not fully trust me. Perhaps he never will, but he shows me how to fashion a bow and arrow out of the reeds at the water's edge.

In turn, I teach him the variety of available plant life in the area. Each day we circle a little bit further out, away from the camp, only speaking when necessary. It is on one of these hunting trips when he asks me a question.

"So, what's the plan?" he says.

We are lying on our stomachs, weapons at the ready, at the top of a ridge line looking out over a meadow. The deer liked to go there during the dusk hours. We hoped to bring at least one back with us.

"What plan?" I reply, keeping my eye steady on the scope.

"You know. The plan. Now that you're here, what's the next step? What will you do?"

It takes me a minute to figure out how to respond to him without scaring off any potential kills hiding at the edge of the meadow. I take a breath, steadying my heart rate before I answer.

"We need to move the camp. It's only a matter of time before there's another breech."

"Where do you think we should move them?" he asks.

I glance sideways toward him. "Back to your parents' place."

The edge of his jawline tenses up. He blinks his eyes rapidly. "Out of the question."

"Ezekiel, we're exposed where we are, and you know it. Your place has water, and we can fortify the fencing. It's the only place we can keep the rest of them safe."

He closes his eyes, resting his forehead on the slight, inclined lift of the ground beneath him. "I don't know if I can go back there, Ash."

Ah, there it is. I give him a minute. The truth is, I've wondered the same about myself.

"I get it," I reply. "But I'll be honest with you. You brought me here to help stop what's been happening to the tribe.

Right now, that's the closest place."

Ezekiel's demeanor changes. His body tenses up as his arms pull tension into his bow. I turn and see the buck stepping tentatively into the field, and I immediately steady my crossbow up to aim.

Before I have a chance to focus my scope onto the deer, I hear the zing snap as Ezekiel's arrow flies to the mark.

"Got him," he whispers with an edge of excitement in his voice. "Let's go skin that sumbitch!"

We stand up, both of us stomping out the tingling in our legs before we head out across the field. At least the victory of the hunt did well to distract Ezekiel from the matter at hand.

We make quick work of the deer, Ezekiel taking the lead on pulling out the stomach before we hack the rest of it into pieces, tying them into a manageable satchel to carry back to the camp. We would all eat well tonight.

Hours later, when the bonfire subsides to crackling embers underneath the charred remains of the night's feasting, he approaches me with his arms crossed.

"Okay," he says.

"Okay, what?" I pick a sliver of meat out of my teeth.

He shrugs. "So we move everyone to the farm. Then what?"

I take a second to observe him. He avoids my direct gaze as he stares out into the night, but he appears earnest enough.

"Once everyone is safe, then I can go after her."

"Yeah? That's the plan?"

"Yeah, that's the plan," I reply. "Not only is she making these super zombies, but she and I have some unfinished business. Pretty sure we can both agree on that."

A twitch of his lip curls into a conspiratorial smile. I don't know if I've ever met anyone more bloodthirsty who hadn't been turned already. But I need him on my side this time.

"She took something from me, something I can never get back. When I went with the others to SeaHaven, that part of me--I thought I could let it go. I thought I could be like everyone else. But I can't. I didn't even know what made me different before, but now I do. And I don't know if I can forgive her for it."

"Hm," he shrugs. "Maybe we're more alike than I thought."

"Maybe so." I follow his gaze into the darkness.

"I still think you're wasting your potential," he says. "I mean, if I could do what you do."

The hair on my arms bristles. "Look, it only works on occasion. I can't just control them all the time. The only real constant is that they leave me alone. But being out here, with them just out of sight, they could be anywhere."

"What's it like?" he asks.

"What's what like?"

"You know. The pull. The mental connection."

"It's hard to say. It's not a pull really. More like an itch."

"Huh." He searches my face, as if able to find some meaning in my features. I give him my best scowl, but it does nothing to dissuade him.

"What are the two of you going on about?" Fairlight approaches, the flames from the dying fire create dark shadows across her face. I glance at Ezekiel, who shakes his head just slightly. He has not yet spoken to her about our plan.

"I was wondering something, Fairlight," I say, not quite ready to show my hand. "Have you considered moving the tribe over the mountains proper, getting everyone closer to the seaside?"

"We'd talked about it a time or two. But we like to stay to the mountains. It gave us the advantage of the traveling routes.

People tend to carry a lot of useful things when they're traveling."

"Do they?" I remember the sheer number of people who traveled with us in the caravan when we left the farm for the last time. Her words serve as a harsh reminder of how we became acquainted.

"It is what it is, Ash," Fairlight says, reading my expression. "We all have to survive. Can't fill your belly on morality, you know."

I opt for dropping the subject. "Of course, now that we've got these super zombies running around, heading east is not a guarantee of safety either."

"So, what are y'all thinking then?" Her eyes shift back and forth between the two of us. I give Ezekiel a slight nod and wait for him to speak.

"We're thinking we go back to my parents' farm," he says. "Reclaim it if we have to, fortify the border fencing. There's a freshwater spring there, and should be provisions left. We can rebuild from there."

"Is it overrun?" Fairlight asks.

"Nothing I can't handle I'm sure," I reply.

To Ezekiel she asks, "And you're okay with this?"

He shuffles his stance, not looking at either one of us. "Yeah. Sure. I mean what other options do we have right now?"

"First light, then," she says. "We'll leave in the morning." Fairlight speaks with the authority of one who is not often questioned.

"I think it would be wise if I went ahead to clear any lingering zombies," I say. "We don't want to lead everyone into ambush after all. We don't know what's there. I go alone and remove the risk."

"By yourself?" Her eyes widen.

"I'm the only one who can."

"I don't know if my people are willing to wait. We've lost so many already."

To my surprise Ezekiel speaks up before I do. "Then you'll want to lower the odds of losing anyone else, right?"

She considers, but not for long. "Fair enough. Give you a day's lead."

"Once it's clear we'll send up the beacon," Ezekiel says. "The plume of smoke from my dad's fire pit."

Fairlight returns to the edge of the fire with the others. Here and there, people drifted away to ready themselves for sleep. Two of the young men would be taking the overnight watch. I see one of them slicing another hunk of venison meat from the fire, carefully handing a slice jabbed on the tip of his knife over to his friend.

"I caught that, you know," I say.

"Caught what?" Ezekiel says.

"You're not coming with me tomorrow. It's not safe for you."

"The hell it is, Ash."

I know full well I won't be able to stop him. The farm was his home for his whole life. He has every right to reclaim it. Of course he'll be coming with me. I never thought otherwise.

"What's not safe?" Alma approaches the two of us.

"We're going back to Eden's farm first thing tomorrow," I reply.

"What? How? I thought it was overrun."

"We'll take it back," Ezekiel says with a casual shrug.

"You two aren't leaving me out," Alma says. "When do we leave?"

I roll my eyes and throw my hands up. "At this point we might as well bring everyone."

"We leave at dawn," Ezekiel replies. "The three of us first, then we signal for the rest, once the property is secure."

"Sounds good. In that case, I guess I'd better go get some sleep."

"Yep. I don't think we're far off, based on what I recall of the landscape," Ezekiel says, "but we've still got quite a hike ahead of us tomorrow."

"Plus, we don't know what we're walking into," I remind him.

"That too."

We go our separate ways. I find my sleeping pallet and scoot in over closer to the fire, pointing my feet towards the warmth.

In the flickering light, I could just make out the shoulders of the two young men already in position to keep watch, finding myself extremely grateful for the night off.

I find it strange, this new dynamic between myself and Ezekiel. We had never truly warmed to one another, but being back here, away from SeaHaven, I feel as if we've developed some kind of understanding between us. How that plays out is yet to be seen.

Seven

We head out the next morning with the sunrise to our backs. Fairlight wakes when we do, ensuring we have a good stash of dried meat, hardtack, and water. Ezekiel insisted we would get there within the day but thanked her for the provisions regardless.

We walk in silence, sticking to the open road as much as possible for the best vantage of the surrounding landscape. Ezekiel took the middle, with Alma and me flanking him on both sides.

It only occurred to me about a mile in that Eden's farm was the last place Alma saw Travis alive. She looks pale. Perhaps she has the same thought. Not until the sun reaches its zenith does anyone speak.

"We should be close now," Ezekiel says. "I know this area from hunting, I think. It's been a while."

"We haven't seen them," I say. "Not one, this whole time."

"Yeah," he says.

Alma remains silent, her eyes scanning the horizon.

"Why do you think that is?" I ask. "Used to be they were everywhere."

He nods but does not speak again.

When we round the bend of the tree line, I recognize the road as the same one I had driven the first time I found their farm, following the plume of smoke rising into the sky. Even now, the scent of meat lingers in the air.

We walk carefully forward, weapons ready. I hold my crossbow. Alma grips in each hand her large hunting knives. Ezekiel carries a machete down at his side, but every muscle in

57

his body tensed at the ready.

Within minutes, the property came into view. I didn't know quite what to expect. The gate and fence still stood, but the chain link had been flattened by multiple footsteps pulling the metal frame down onto the ground, curved like a sadistic smile.

With careful, measured steps, we cross over the fallen fence. There still appear to be no creatures in sight. The house stands vacant, the door hanging open and the windows dull.

I smelled blood in the air.

Blood, and terror.

"They came from that way," Ezekiel says, pointing toward the western edge of the forest. "Too many to count."
Alma and I both lower our weapons, standing side by side as he speaks.

"My mother saw them first through the kitchen window. She spent so much time in that kitchen. I heard her call out to Dad, out in the garden."

"Where were you?" Alma asks quietly.

"I had just come back from the springs." He gestured toward the path leading to the forest's edge on the other side of the farm. "I had a couple of gallons of water draped over my shoulders, so I wasn't moving very quickly. I heard her shout before I saw them. But there were so many of them. They looked like a thick wall, just a mass of them. I knew as soon as I saw them..." His eyes went distant.

"He didn't hear me. His hearing had pretty much gone in the past year. I shouted as loud as I could, thinking maybe if he could make it to the house... They breeched the fence. So many bodies pressing against it. The thing crumbled like paper. Even then, he didn't hear them."

He paused. We neared the warped, wooden porch, careful to avoid the shards of glass scattered upon the ground from the broken windows.

"Let me," I say, moving forward onto the first step. They both followed a few feet behind me as I stepped through the door, walking to the center of the room.

"Look," I whisper, nudging my toe against the leg of the dining chair. "This is where we had that humdinger of an argument."

"Yeah," he replies. "I still say I'm right."

Alma and I exchange a silent glance, and she rolls her eyes with a smirk. We move forward.

Now and again, one of us would find some relic that was once part of this warm household. A half-empty coffee mug sitting at the table, a framed photograph of the two of them fallen to the floor, from the shelf in the hall. We made our way into the kitchen. Just as Ezekiel had said, this room had been Eden's domain.

She had fed us, and to her, that food equaled care, perhaps even love. This place had been a way station, welcoming anyone who needed help or sought a better way of life. We had moved through the whole house by this point, and by all accounts it seemed empty, but I still feel uneasy.

Ezekiel made his way toward the bookshelf, placing his foot over one of the floorboards, pressing against the surface with intention, moving from one to the other.

"Ah, here it is," he says.

"What is it?" Alma asks.

"The panic room." He reaches down and pulls up the board, revealing a metal handle connected to a segment of the floor, an inset trap door disguised into the hardwood. In that instance, I understand the source of my disquiet.

"Ezekiel, wait!" I call out, but he had already pulled open the heavy door.

The sound and smell rush from the inside of the poorly ventilated space. The dead. Rather, the undead.

I felt them too, an assault on my mind as much as my senses. The expression on Ezekiel's face revealed to me what he saw down below.

The sounds crying out from within sounded all too familiar. Alma gasped, her hand flying to her mouth before she rushed back out the front door, her last meal escaping her body without ceremony.

Ezekiel took a step back, his breath quick and shallow. He had always been distant towards me, but I sensed for a while that his emotional stuntedness had more to do with his personality before the Fall than the apocalypse itself. But now, I see on his face what he had to do may be too difficult, even for him.

"Ezekiel," I say, my voice thick in my throat.

He picks up the bow strapped to his back, bringing it forward and aiming it down into the underground space. I step forward, placing my hand on his arm.

When he looks up, I see the dampness in his eyes, teeth clenched and beads of sweat sheened across his forehead.

"Let me," I say, as gently as I can. "You don't want to do this."

He pauses, his eyes darting back and forth as he looks into mine.

"Please," I whisper, holding his gaze.

He struggles for just a moment before finally relenting, lowering his bow and taking a step backward. I move forward, not at all excited about what I am about to see.

When I gaze down into the panic room, I see two familiar faces drawn by death and time, peering back up at me.

These creatures, who had once been Eden and Abraham, gnashed their teeth with a ferociousness rivaling their kindness in life.

Abraham's shoulder bore a bloody gash, shredded skin ripped open and hanging against exposed bone. Eden had a similar wound on her arm, the only difference being hers had been bandaged.

She must have been bitten first. Perhaps Abraham had attempted to tend to her after they made their way inside. From what I knew of them, neither one would leave the side of the other, regardless of the cost.

I step down into the darkened room, gripping the knife hard in my hand. The shuffle in place, eyeing me with alien hunger.

Everything about them looks different. Eden's bloody jaw hangs slack, her arms dangling at her sides. Abraham no longer holds the slight bend he had always carried when he walked.

These things before me carried none of their mannerisms. Each time I take a step down, I watch their actions. They make no move towards me.

Finally, I stand before them, just the three of us. Glancing back up the stairs, I see no sign of Ezekiel.

Good. He doesn't need to be around for this part.

"Okay, you two," I say quietly. "I'm here for one reason. My friends, Eden and Abraham, are to be put to rest today. Now it just so happens that you two bear a striking resemblance to them, but I can promise you one thing. You ain't them. I'm going to do this and neither one of you are going to stand in my way. Do we have an agreement?"

They shuffle in place, giving me nothing more than a distracted, milky-eyed gaze.

"Good," I reply. "So, we understand each other."

I take a deep breath, doing my best to ignore the familiarity of their faces.

"You're not them," I whisper.

No sense in putting this off. I raise my arm, bringing it in from the side.

First Abraham. The blade sinks into the base of his skull without much resistance. He goes down fast, his old knees buckling the moment I sever his cerebellum.

Next, Eden. She drops immediately, crumbling next to her husband.

With her forehead landing in such a way that it is touching his arm, they almost look as if they could be sleeping. I'll have to have one of the others help me carry them out. For now, I adjust them, side by side, arms crossed, eyes closed.

When I went outside, I find Ezekiel and Alma sitting side by side on the steps of the front porch. He turns to me as I join them, his eyes wide and questioning.

"It's done," I say.

He nods, his lips pressed together in a thin line. "Well then. We've got some work to do, I guess. There's a flatbed wheelbarrow in the warehouse, Ash. Why don't you grab that? Alma and I will bring up the bodies."

It only occurs to me in that moment that he may have some difficulty with what I had just done. "Ezekiel, I'm sorry--"

He raises his hand. "Ash, I don't-- Was it quick?"

"Yes, it was."

"Thank you," he replies.

The pyre remains from Travis' memorial. Alma falls silent when she sees it. We build it back up to account for the bodies of Eden and Abraham, placing the large pieces of wood against the rock base.

Hand in hand, we watch as their flesh curled inward within the flames, thin as paper. It takes hours, but in the end, the embers die down, nothing left of them but hollow bones.

All that remains of the daylight is a distant orange sheen on the Western horizon beyond the trees. We head back to the farmhouse to prepare for the night. We have a lot of work to do in the coming days.

Eight

Alma sits alone on the porch swing, one leg drawn up underneath her, her dark hair swept over one shoulder. Her olive skin appears pallid and her eyes reddened.

"Ezekiel's already out there," she says, without looking at me. "He said to tell you."

"Yeah, okay." I see him several yards away, pulling the vines away from the fallen fence line.

"Ash, wait." Alma sniffles, running a hand over her nose. "Um…"

"What's going on?" I ask, sitting down on the porch step. "You okay?"

"No, I'm not. I'm pregnant." She still has not looked at me once. The words take me by surprise.

"How can that be?"

"It's been three months since Travis died," she says.

"Oh, Alma…" I murmur, unsure if I should finish with "I'm sorry" or "congratulations."

"The thing is," she continues, "I knew it right away. We were going to run off together, maybe find a place kind of like this one. Just the two of us. We figured we'd already lost everything. What's the worst that could happen? But then…"

"We went to the compound," I say. "Oh, I'm so sorry. If I had known…"

"It's not your fault, Ash. You can't blame yourself for everything, you know. He's the one who left his window down. So stupid…" Her voice catches. She rubs her cheek with the palm of her hand.

"What are you going to do?" I ask quietly, unsure if the words are right.

"I don't know yet. That's why I wanted to come with you. I wanted a minute on my own, away from Rose. Just to get my head clear, you know?"

"Yeah."

"Hey, listen," Alma says. "Don't tell... well, don't tell anyone just yet. But I wanted to say it out loud, just once. Okay?"

"Okay. I won't."

"Thanks, Ash." Her eyes find their way to me, meeting mine at last. "I'm glad we're friends."

"Me too, Alma."

"You'd better get going before Ezekiel has a breakdown."

"What's with her?" Ezekiel says, nodding his head towards Alma. "It's not like her to sit out on stuff like this."

"She's... not feeling well," I reply.

"Huh." His eyes dart out toward the forest on the other side of the fence line. "How many are there?" he asks.

"How many what?" I reply, focused on lifting the outer edge of the chain link.

"How many zombies? I'm sure the woods are crawling with them. I'm surprised we haven't seen any yet."

I pause for a moment, reaching out my mind into the forest, searching. "There aren't any."

"What do you mean?"

"I mean, I haven't sensed a single one for miles now. Except for yesterday."

"Right." He cleared his throat and turned his attention back to his task.

"Ezekiel, I didn't mean--"

"No, it's okay. I mean, it is what it is."

"Yeah. Yeah, I guess so."

We work in silence for a while, falling into an easy rhythm. I pull the fencing up to vertical. He hammers the posts into position. We walk five steps forward and repeat.

"Where are they all?" he asks. "They can't have all cleared out to the mountains. I mean we saw half a dozen a week sometimes up there. Those fast ones especially. I don't know. Something just doesn't add up."

"Yeah, so let's get to the meat of it, Eze. Why did you bring me out here?"

"She's got some kind of beacon at the compound," he says.

"Beacon?"

"Yeah. I think it's some kind of sound thing. Like a frequency. It draws them. That's where they are I think."

"If she can do that, why is she targeting your people?"

"That's what we don't know."

"And that's what you want me to find out," I say.

He does not answer, but I see it in his eyes.

"You know, when I was out west, I saw them roaming in hordes all over the place. I hardly ever saw them in smaller groups or on their own. It almost seemed like they were drawn to each other somehow. Maybe she's found a way to tap into that."

"Could be," he says.

"Look, Ezekiel," I glance back towards Alma, still curled up on the porch swing, her knees drawn to her chest. "I've been thinking. Maybe I should go the rest of the way..."

"On your own?" he asks, completing my thought.

"Yeah. You and Alma can get this place up to working condition. Bring in the others. Make sure everyone is safe. I'll go ahead, try to get a lay of the place. We have no idea what's happened since we broke in and got everyone out."

"Why do I think there's more to it than that?" he says with a smirk.

"Because there is."

"Unfinished business." His smirk curls into a grin.

I ignore his obvious delight. We continue to pull the chain link around the next metal bar. He passes the fence up and over.

"Yeah," he says. "I think that's a good idea. As long as you're up for it."

"I'm sure I am."

I hadn't told him about the basement, how it felt walking those few minutes through the horde of zombies, their cold, dank bodies shuffling all around me. Especially the mind connection, that old familiar tug, feeling it click into place to where I know I can control them.

I didn't tell him that I also feel their hunger. They, no matter how grotesque or horrifying they appear, are still in there, somehow.

I leave after lunch. The first layer of the fence has been completed, and Alma says she feels well enough to help with the rest. Ezekiel finds us some preserved chicken and tomato concoction in the storage pantry. We eat it cold, straight out of the jars. It tastes rather salty, but it has calories and I have a long journey ahead of me.

"I wish I could come with you," Alma says, wrapping her arms around my shoulders.

"I wouldn't let you anyway."

"Did you tell him about... you know?"

"No, I didn't."

"Be careful out there," Ezekiel says as he approaches from the house. He hands me a knife holster containing a couple of the blades he procured from the household stash.

I position this around my waist, careful that I still have

access to my crossbow and backpack slung across my back. I leave without much ado. I know the two of them can handle themselves. Besides, I can sense there isn't a zombie for miles.

It feels good to be alone in a strange way. Before I ran into Marcus and Rachel that one day, I'd been alone for the most part of four years. Now, after everything that has happened, I nearly consider SeaHaven as my home. The people there have created more than just survival. They have created a life.

But this solitude has its own benefits. I like being out here. The mere freedom of not having to look out for anyone else already makes me feel unencumbered.

Not until nightfall, when I set up camp, do I realize I am not fully alone. Just at the edges of my mind I sense them, one or two, close by. More further out.

They have no interest in me so far. I let my mind wander, ruminating on the day I had found my way back to the laboratory. The place where I had found the picture of me, a smiling child standing next to Dr. Donovan, beaming down at me like any proud parent. At least, carrying the semblance of one.

I still have the photograph, along with a few others, dog-eared and tucked into my backpack. Children standing in a row, in a classroom. A scrap of a sunset.

The sound of a scuffle brings me out of my thoughts. Movement up ahead in the trees and shrubbery.

Dead movement.

Shuffling, dragging.

I reach out with my mind. It only takes a second to connect, tucked in there behind the tree. I tease it out, goading the creature towards me. After several seconds it emerges out of the trees. A girl. Not much older than myself.

"There you are," I whisper. "Hi there." She does not move

fast. I loosen my grip on the hilt of the knife as she shuffles forward. I can sense she means me no harm.

Yet.

On one foot she wears a tattered, worn Mary Jane buckled around dusty stockings. Her other foot is bare, her toes black with caked blood and dirt. The slight life from the heel of her shoe causes her to move with an exaggerated lurch, more so than her already unnatural gate of the undead.

"What's your name, I wonder?"

Her only response is that dead-eyed stare. Her face remains largely uninjured. She wears a yellow sundress, ripped at the shoulder, exposing a still intact tattoo of a flying bird. Her mud-caked hair could be any color underneath the grime.

"Alright then. Maybe your name is Penny. Can I call you Penny?"

Her only reply, a mindless stare.

I continue onward. She shuffles along behind me, her head kinked over to the side. Watching her as we travel, I see no evidence as to how she could have died. No marks other than the usual symptoms of decay, sunken eyes, bluish lips stretched across skeletal teeth.

She walked along a bit behind me for a few miles, tethered by our tentative mental connection.

She shuffles past me, speeding up her uneven gait.

"What are you up to?" I muse. Her action prompts me to release my end of the mental hold just a bit, enough to give her some independent movement. She veers off the path and into the trees. I follow a handful of feet behind her through the forest.

If I had been in front, I would have pushed aside the branches, but this lifeless creature just sludges forward as branches tug at her clothing and skin. I stay close enough to keep her in sight up ahead.

"Where are we going, Penny?"

Her answer arrives when we step into a clearing. She slows, but does not stop. Overhead, I spot the birds circling against the patch of sky, having spotted the deer lying dead across the grass, the same that beckons Penny.

"You hungry?" I ask.

She launches herself into the creature, diving into the guts of the dead beast up to her elbows, shameless in her consumption. For a split second, I feel what she feels, the hunger and the promise of feeling satiated.

I let go, breaking the mental connection and sitting on the ground, crossing my legs. She gorges herself, scraping the meat and viscera into her mouth.

Her performance is something I have never seen this close before. I know they feel wildly hungry nearly always, but seeing that hunger in action puts it into a new perspective.

Another small clutch of zombies emerges from the forest, about a half-dozen moving around me as if I am a rock in a stream. They lurch towards the remains of the deer, ignoring each other and settling into their own patch corner to feed, smacking and ripping flesh off the bones.

I find I am enjoying the solitude. Even though Ezekiel and I had formed a tentative truce, it feels nice to be away from that.

We got along, but that was about the extent of it.

My mind wanders. Blue sky, purple heather, the wind in the tall green grass.

Something wanders in the trees, just beyond the clearing. I sense it walking along, circling the edge, hesitant to approach.

Not a zombie, but something else, an animal of some kind.

Whatever it is, it does not seem to pose a threat just now, and within a few seconds, it moves away.

The zombies begin to shuffle off, one by one, the deer

stripped to the bone. They wander into the forest. Penny, the first to arrive, is the last to move from her feast.

I can see in her movement the momentary feeling of satiation. Her tattered cotton dress is now soaked with blood, and the bright red circle around her mouth gives her a clownish appearance. Blood coats her arms, dripping from her fingertips as she moves.

She stands in stiff jerky movements, before following the others into the trees. My presence has apparently been forgotten. I rise and follow.

Moving through the woods, I find myself making far more noise than they do. I know stealth, having lived out here for the majority of my life, it being as much a survival requirement as air and water.

But even so, the branches break and crack as I move through them. The half-dozen who had feasted on that deer are now joined by others coalescing into a larger horde, one by one.

I do my best to keep a good distance between us. I don't like being around large groups of them. It makes my brain feel… slimy.

But I keep on, careful of my steps, slowing down and speeding up to keep pace with them. Even with the distance between us, several yards at least, I sense them, more and more, the longer we travel.

They begin to vanish, I realize. Up ahead, somewhere. I don't see it until I nearly fall over the edge, the huge cavern, a deep slope jettisoning out into thin air.

The hillside leads down to the massive horde. I stare down at them, collected in the natural indent of the earth, hundreds of them, unable to escape.

I take a step toward the edge, drawn to them in a way I cannot place. I squint down and spot Penny in the crowd. There she is, yellow dress, clown face, and one dusty black shoe.

She doesn't frighten me. None of them do. If I joined them, they would all just ignore me. It would be the safest place for me, really.

All of a sudden, I hear someone calling my name. I turn and squint against the bright sky, trying to determine if I had imagined it. I see someone running toward me, but they are just a silhouette. I can't make them out.

"Ash!" the voice calls again.

That's when I realize they are being chased. A clutch is moving after them. Whoever this is, Ezekiel I'm assuming, they're in danger.

This isn't like him, to get stuck in this kind of situation. The clutch behind him, they move fast, motivated by hunger. He is in obvious danger.

"Ash!" he calls once more, finally clearing the glare. I see him. I see his face.

"Thorn!" Dammit! "What are you-- Thorn!"

I run towards him. I have to get to him before they do. I can't let him die. I reach out with my mind, struggling to push them back, to slow them down even just a little bit. I lean forward and tackle him at a full run, knocking him to the ground.

"What the hell, Ash--"

"Shut up and stay down!" I snap through clenched teeth.

I plant myself on top of him, masking his body with my own, arms and hands clutching wrist to wrist, elbow to elbow. He lies flat on his back, face to face with me, stunned.

The feet shuffle past us. He falls silent as he realizes the danger he had escaped.

I sense unrest from them. I hold my breath that my presence is enough to shield Thorn from their interest. Fresh blood, coursing through his veins, calls to them. I know it does.

73

Finally, they pass, vanishing over the edge into the canyon. I don't move until the very last one tumbles over.

I relax, pulling myself off of him, letting go of his wrists and letting him sit up. He rubs his hands against his wrists.

"Why did you do that?" he asks.

"I just saved your life!" I snap. "What are you even doing here?"

He glances away, crossing his legs and resting his elbows against his knees. A shock of hair falls across his forehead, into his eyes. Irritation rises within me.

"I asked you a question, Thorn."

He glances my way. His expression remains unreadable.

"If I hadn't been here, they would have eaten you, you know. *Eaten you*. That's not even a metaphor. They would have literally eaten you. Do you even get that?"

"Yeah, Ash. Yeah, I do."

"I don't know that you do." I turn away, brushing the sweat off my forehead, raking my fingers across my scalp. "So, what *are* you doing here?"

"I followed you. I've been shadowing you since SeaHaven."

"What? Why?"

"I had to see you."

"What?"

He shrugs. "I didn't like how we left things. I hate fighting with you."

"You came all this way just to apologize?"

"Maybe. So what?"

"Dammit, Thorn. You could have been killed," I reply softly. I don't know if I like the way I feel right now with him looking at me like that.

He stands up, brushing the dirt off his legs. I let him take my hand to pull me to my feet. "What's over there anyway?"

"Come on." I motion him over. He gives a low whistle at the sight of them.

"How many are down there do you think?" he asks.

"Hundreds at least."

"What do they want?"

"They want to eat," I reply. "That's all they ever want."

Thorn turns to me, peering at me the way he does. My heart still races from the adrenaline of the close call moments ago. I find I want to ask him something, but I cannot form any words.

I kiss him.

Square on the mouth, one hand wrapped around his head, holding him steady, fingers curled through his hair. Eyes closed.

I had only ever read about it. So far, he is the only one I ever wanted to try it with. The best part is he kisses me back.

His hands finding their way to my hips, thumbs hooked into my belt loops, pulling me into him. He is whole and perfect, and I realize I don't want anything else.

"Look," he says when we finally part a bit. "I know I'm not very good at being out here, but I'm coming with you to the lab. I know my way around there. I can help you."

I take a step back, trying to catch my breath without being so obvious about it. "Okay," I say. "I'll be glad of the company to be honest."

He replies with a half-grin.

"But as long as we're out here, you do exactly as I say. You got it?" I keep my glare steady.

"Got it," he replies with a nod. His fingers curl into mine. "I don't want to make a habit of you needing to save my life."

"You'd better not. We still have a lot of daylight, you know."

"Lead the way." He gestures. I try to hide my smile as we

make our way, hand in hand, back to the road.

Nine

Back at the road, the landscape remains relatively zombie free. We walk side by side on each side of the double yellow line in the middle of the asphalt.

"You shouldn't have come, you know," I say. "You could have been killed."

"I get that," he replies with a smile. "But I couldn't leave things the way we did. I don't like us being mad at each other."

"Yeah. Me either." I return his smile.

"I'm sorry about what I said. I didn't mean it."

"No, it's true though. I am weird."

"Maybe so. But not for that reason," he grins.

I shove him in the arm. He laughs in response. Against the horizon I spot the distant walls of the compound, a small gray blemish on an otherwise perfect landscape.

The birds go silent. The once cheerful surroundings become desolate. The trees to the left of us become bare, spindly branches reaching to the empty sky.

"Why is it so quiet?" he asks.

"Animals sometimes go quiet when predators are close by," I reply.

"What about--?" He stops, averting his eyes away from me.

"What were you going to say?"

"No, don't worry about it. Never mind."

"Thorn!" I stop and cross my arms until he looks at me. "You can ask me. It's okay."

He glances to the ground between us. "What about you?" he asks. "Can you sense when there's predators around?"

"I see." I lower my face in an attempt to hide my smirk.

"Yeah, I kind of can."

"And?"

"We're getting closer. They're close, but not a threat just now."

He glances around. "The compound is close. I think maybe another couple of miles."

I hand him a bottle of water from my backpack. "Here. We need to nail down some kind of plan. You know the lay out of the place better than I do. What do you recommend?"

"That depends on what you're looking for. What's your goal?"

"Recon. I need to get an idea of what she's doing. We know she's taking healthy people. I'd like to find out why. I mean," I glance back toward the ravine, "we have an idea, but I want to know the specifics. What is she doing to them, and how?"

"Yeah." Thorn glances to the ground before returning his gaze to me. "That's valid. I mean--"

"Shh!" I motion for him to keep silent.

Something moves in the distance. I scour the horizon and the surrounding tree line. I know I heard something, felt something. Just the smallest shift in the atmosphere, but I see nothing. When I turn back to Thorn, he too is scanning the surroundings, his eyes darting back and forth.

"Maybe it's nothing," I say.

"Don't be so sure," he replies. "Look." He motions toward something in the distance, a creature lurching with little motivation, about a mile away.

"Well spotted, Thorn," I say, flashing him a smile.

"Never doubt yourself, Ash," he replies with a grin.

The zombie is near enough now that I can make out the bloodstained yellow dress.

"Penny!" I say. "How the hell did she get out of the

ravine?"

"You've named them? You can't be serious."

"Just the one. For whatever reason, this one seems to have some kind of attachment to me."

"She was in the horde back there?"

"Yeah."

"I wonder what she wants?" Thorn muses.

"Probably nothing. I'm sure it's just a coincidence."

"Of course." He smirks with a side eye.

"Come on. We've still got plenty of daylight left."

Thorn watches Penny out of the corner of his eye as we make our way down the road once more. We are close enough now that I can see the gaping hole in the side of the building.

We had rammed Abraham's truck through it to get everyone out. Unfortunately, that's how we lost Travis. I scan the top of the building, the upper walls where Dr. Donovan had brought me to show me what surrounded the landscape around the compound, chock full of zombies.

This time however, the same space remains vacant. Even when I reach out mentally, I sense nothing. The compound is empty, as far as I can tell.

"What's wrong?" Thorn asks, watching my face.

"I don't know yet. Something's not right though. We should get off the road before we go any further."

He follows me silently. We move through the trees, trying to make as little noise as possible. We move parallel to the edge of the compound, glimpsing now and then through the trees, searching for any kind of movement.

"Anything?" Thorn whispers.

"No. Wait..." I hear them before I see anything, thundering, distant hoofbeats against the ground.

Following the sound, we emerge into a clearing, a wide

swath of land devoid of trees. A wooden fence crosses in front of us. There in the distance, I see the raised dust of the herd against the horizon.

"I wonder what's got them so worked up," he says.

"I think I know." A man appears across the field, carrying a large bucket. Thorn and I duck to the ground to keep out of his sight. He walks along the outer edge of the fence, calling to the horses in a melodic voice, rising to a high-pitched whistle. The horses near, their heads bobbing in anticipation of being fed.

When he empties the bucket into the trough, that's when we realize what we are seeing. The contents spill out, huge bloody rodents, split down the stomach.

The horses line up, their noses already furrowing into the offered delights. A breeze shifts towards us, bringing with it a tinge of the unmistakable smell of decay.

"Are those…?"

"Zombie horses," I complete the sentence for him.

"Unbelievable."

We stay where we are, silently watching the man finish up his duties, whistling as he goes.

"Watch to see where he goes," Thorn murmurs. "There should be a tunnel leading into the compound."

"Tunnel?"

"Yeah. We used to have safety drills when I was a kid. They would shuffle all of us into these big hallways and lock the doors on either side. My dad figured out that one end had to lead to the woods outside the compound."

"Safety drills?"

"Yeah. They stopped when I was about five, I think. Apparently, there hadn't been any security breech, so they didn't see a need for them anymore." His eyes search along the edge of the forest where the man had disappeared. The horses remained happily eating, their ears flicking and muzzles stained red. "I can't believe I remember that. I hadn't thought about those drills in years. The alarm went off and we had ten minutes to get to the safety areas."

"Ten minutes. That's not much time. What happened if someone didn't make it?"

"They got locked out."

"She has no limits."

"No. She really doesn't." His gaze returns to the field, focusing on the horses. "Can you feel them? Like you do the others?"

"A little bit. It's different though. They feel more… animal. If that makes sense."

"It does. A little." He slides his gaze over to me.

"Do you think it's clear?" I ask.

"Yeah. I'm pretty sure I can get us to the head of the tunnel. We just have to skirt around the edge of this fence."

"Let me go first," I say.

"Ash, wait. You can't--"

I raise my hand to quiet him. Raising up, I step out from behind our hiding place. If anyone is watching, they would see me out in the open.

I wait, but nothing happens. No blaze of weapons from an unseen tower, nothing. I step forward to the edge of the paddock.

"Ash, wait. We don't know anything about those creatures out there."

"Hush," I wave him quiet. "I have to try. But I need you to stay quiet. We don't know how they could react to you. Your presence might irritate them."

He falls silent. I walk forward slowly, calling to the horses in a quiet voice. Over the years on my own, I managed to pick up enough knowledge regarding equine behavior to break and ride one if I need to. However, zombie horses... This is something new.

Ever so carefully, I climb over the wooden fencing into the open field. Most of the horses had already wandered towards the middle of the field. My presence draws their attention. I reach out my hand, beckoning. The two closest to me, still a few yards away, start to make a sound close to a curious whinnie, but lower, deeper, a ghostly moan, like a crying child.

"Hey there," I murmur. "It's alright. I'm not going to hurt you. Easy, now... Easy."

One of them nears, a mare, taking tentative steps toward my outstretched hand. The creature appears much like any other horse for the most part, other than the tell-tale features of the undead.

The creature's eyes appear glazed over, milky white. Ears tattered but clean. The mane appeared to be trimmed to a short ruff, exposing the decayed flesh of her neck. Bare, greenish-gray muscle peeking out between torn, matted skin.

"Easy," I whisper. She is close enough now I can touch her nose. One inch at a time, I place my palm against the cold bare skin of her muzzle.

As soon as we make contact, I feel her inner turmoil surging through both of us like an open dam. This dead, lifeless creature still carries an animal rage deep inside, much like the insatiable hunger of the human zombies.

"Oh, I know this rage," I whisper. I know this. What did she do to you, Beauty?"

In a strange moment of normalcy, she nuzzles my hand, behaving much like a regular horse. Her flesh feels cold and dead, but I feel that strange spark within her still.

"Ash?" Thorn's voice interrupts the silence. The horse tosses her head, a sharp whinny escapes her. Her ears flatten against her head. I turn to find him standing at the edge of the fence.

"Back up! She's spooked!" I snap.

"I don't think she's spooked," he says, but he recedes into the shadow of the woods behind him. As soon as he is out of sight, she calms.

"See? No one here will hurt you," I murmur. "Don't you worry. I'll get you out of here. You and all your friends there. One way or another."

Making my way back, I find Thorn just inside the tree line, squinting through the trees toward the spot where the man had vanished.

"You're right, you know."

"About what?" he asks, turning my way.

"She wasn't spooked."

"Oh?"

"No. I could feel her when I touched her nose. I felt what she felt."

"And?" He raised one eyebrow.

"Your presence taunted her. What she felt was not fear. It was hunger."

His face goes pale but only for a moment. He swallows and gestures forward. "Shall we?"

I take his outstretched hand, reveling in the warmth of his skin against mine, warm, vibrant, living flesh, fingertips grazing against my palm. I cannot help but smile, just a little bit.

We follow the tree line until we reach the trough. The farm hand had vanished, but we spot the open door to the tunnels, a garish metal hatch, still standing open. A wheelbarrow carrying a pair of leather gloves and garden sheers is parked a few feet from the entrance.

Thorn holds his finger to his lips, gesturing for silence.

The man may still be close by. I nod.

He steps forward, closing the gap between us. With his free hand, he brushes his fingertips along a strand of my hair, briefly skimming his thumb across my lower lip. I feel my cheeks flush at the gesture. The silent moment speaks volumes.

I let him lead but reach forward with my mind, finding the passages empty. Hand in hand, we duck into the tunnel entrance, slipping through the darkness of the hallway.

Up ahead I see flickering lights, barely illuminating the door, leading into what I can guess is the main area of the compound. This place must be a maze based on the length of this tunnel alone.

At the far end, we find another doorway, standing open, leading off the hall into a small room, one wall covered in television monitors. A well-worn, rolling chair sits akimbo in the center of the room. A side table contains a plate and the leavings of a sandwich, and a half-empty bottle of water. Thorn and I exchange a look. The man could come back at any moment.

The monitors each flicker grainy images between a number of areas on the compound, some of which I recognize. The restaurant where I had met Rose stands abandoned, the service window just an empty frame. In another, I spot the room where I had first woken up and the dumbwaiter which had taken me further into the belly of the beast.

"Look, there," Thorn whispers.

He points to the screen in the top right corner. The movement of black and white shapes reveal themselves and I recognize her. Dr. Margaret Donovan, still wearing that white lab coat. She stands with her back to the camera, leaning over a microscope, picking up a vial, moving here and there through her laboratory.

"What do you think she's doing?" I whisper.

"Hard to say. What I want to know is, where are the others?"

"Others?"

"This place used to be filled with people. Scientists, families, children. We only rescued about a third of the people here altogether, when we did. Everyone else would have pulled back into the panic rooms. So where are they?"

He has a point. My eyes never leave the image of Dr. Donovan in her lab. Something seems… off. But I can't place what it is. She's alone in there, but she carries herself with a purpose, never turning toward the camera, consumed with her research.

"Ash, are you okay?"

As soon as he speaks the words, a sharp pain stabs behind my eyes, attacking my brain with such a ferocity that I cry out, pressing my palms against my temples. With my eyes squeezed shut, I feel Thorn's arm around my shoulders as I lean into him.

"Let's get you out of here," he says.

I can't open my eyes. Even the dim flickering of the fluorescent lights penetrates through my closed eyelids. I sense him leading me quickly along the passage to outside. Everything hurts.

Stepping out into the natural light does me no favors. My knees nearly buckle beneath me.

"Can you make it?" he asks.

"I'll make do," I reply.

"Hey!" The man from before, the farm hand, emerges from what sounds like the other side of the hatch. "Stop right there!"

I hear a light clicking sound, a gun being cocked. Between my pain and the light affecting my vision, the only thing I can sense clearly are the emotions of the creature. The mare. I hear the middling sound of her screaming in the field.

"Thorn," I mutter. "Get me to the horse."

"Ash, you can't mean--"

"Get me there! If you keep close enough to me, I can shield you from her. It's our only hope right now."

Without hesitation, he scoops me up into his arms. I tuck my head into his shoulder, trying to become as small as possible. We dart through the trees. A sound of thunder explodes behind us. The man is firing at us.

We make it to the fence. Thorn sets me down. I stumble forward, finding her at the edge of the field, as if waiting for us.

When I place my palm against her neck, the pain subsides, but only a little, enough to offer a reprieve. One foot on the lower rung of the fence, I kick myself up and over, clutching the tufts of her mane to steady myself.

I grasp Thorn by the forearm and pull him up behind me. He clutches my waist, his breath hot on my neck, and we dart forward, turning away from the fence and toward the far side of the field.

She runs. I lean forward, keeping my palms flat against her neck. The skin-to-skin contact seems to calm both of us somehow.

She is not pleased with Thorn's presence, but I managed to control her through this bizarre mental connection. Hopefully long enough to get us out of here.

The man shouts again, another explosion ringing out behind us. She breaks into a gallop, leaping over the fence and stone wall at the opposite side.

We are free. She continues to gallop with unending stamina, carrying us forward into the barren landscape.

Ten

Her speed never wavers, the landscape rushing past us.

"Ash," Thorn says, his voice sounding thin and reedy. Even with the wind rushing past us and the migraine fighting for purchase in my brain, his words caught me off guard. "Ash, I've been hit."

He leans against me hard, his head and shoulders falling slack against my back. I can feel him losing consciousness based on how loose his grasp is around my waist. I lean forward toward the horse's neck to allow him some semblance of support.

"Come on, Mare," I whisper into the horse's tattered ear. "Just a little bit further."

We aim towards the farm. I know Ezekiel will be there, and if anyone knows how to deal with a gunshot wound, it's him. I only hope the man is not following us.

As we distance from the compound, the pain in my head lessens considerably. My vision clears finally, and I am able to focus on the road ahead.

Mare continues to gallop at full throttle, as if running from hell itself. Thorn's full body weight leans on me and I feel sure he has passed out. We round the bend, and the gravel road leading into the farm comes into view.

"Ezekiel!" I call out as loud as I can. "Open the gate!"

I pulled the horse to a stop, unsure how Ezekiel might react to her. I certainly didn't want any harm to come to her. I tug gently on her mane, just enough to get her attention. She slows, pulling up short, her front hooves stamping against the rocky ground.

Ezekiel pulls open the gates, one at a time. In the distance, I spot Alma standing on the porch watching us.

"Don't come too close," I say.

The task of getting Thorn off the horse turns out to be a bit of a project. I can't turn around enough to get a good grip around his shoulders.

He slides off as I pull his shoulders towards me, landing hard on the ground. I lead the horse away, doing my best to calm her.

As soon as I get the horse clear, Ezekiel rushes to him, pulling Thorn to his feet and guiding him toward the gate. Mare takes a few steps into the darkness of the surrounding forest. She stops and peers back at me.

I jog toward the gates, pulling them each closed behind me. I meet up to Ezekiel and pull Thorn's free arm over my shoulder to help stabilize him.

Ezekiel glances over Thorn's head and catches my eye. "So, what was that back there?"

"Zombie horse," I reply dryly.

He nods. "Yeah. That's what I thought. Seems about right. Where'd you find her?"

"I'm pretty sure we've got other things to worry about right now."

We lay Thorn down on the grass near the firepit. I pull off my jacket, placing it between his wound and the ground.

"What do we do?" I ask.

"Hold your hands like this, and put pressure on it right here." Ezekiel takes my hand, pressing my palm against the bullet hole in Thorn's shoulder.

The hot blood presses against my palm, his life force seeping out between my fingers.

"Is he going to be okay?" I ask.

"It's too soon to tell. Alma, bring me the first aid kit and one of the blankets from the panic room."

"We need the others. Fairlight has people who would know how to handle this. At least, she used to. Maybe she still does."

Alma arrives with the supplies. The two of them crouch on either side of his prone form, working around me to clean and dress the area.

"Do you want me to go?" I ask, feeling wildly out of place. "I can go and get Fairlight. Bring her here. That was the plan anyway, right?"

"I can go," Alma says. "That way you can stay with-"

"No, I'll do it," I reply, suddenly anxious to get out of there. "It's faster to take the horse and I'm the only one who can ride her."

Alma's eyes furrow, but Ezekiel backs me up. "She's right. Besides, I'll need you to help me stabilize him. Ash, go. Don't worry about the others. Just get Fairlight here as quick as you can."

I risk a quick glance at Thorn, lying prone on his back. The fabric Alma pressed against his wounds already tinged red between her taut fingers. His face appears pale, eyes fluttering as he struggles for consciousness.

"Ash," Ezekiel says, pulling my attention back. "Go."
I nod, heading back toward the gate.

Half an hour at a full gallop gets me to where they are. I leave the horse a good distance from the camp. She just does not do well around regular people, and to tell the truth, I don't much care for it either. So, I tuck away my impatience and go the rest of the way on foot.

"Where's Fairlight?" I ask as one of the women spots me approaching. The children scurry around us, and she sends one of them to fetch her.

"What's happened?" the woman asks, worry lines etching her forehead. "Ezekial, is he--?"

"He's fine, but Thorn's been shot."

"And who is Thorn?" Fairlight asks as she approaches.

"He's one of the community from SeaHaven. He came with all of us the first time we crossed, from the compound."

"I see. One of the ones you rescued."

"Yes." I step close to her, turning my shoulder so only she and I can speak. "Please we need to hurry."

"How bad is it?"

"It's bad."

Fairlight turns to the woman, speaking to her in quick clipped words. "In the first aid cache, go and get me the alfalfa, and the Yarrow root. Bring all of it as quick as you can. And the bandages."

"I have a horse of sorts," I say. "But I'm the only one who can control her. If you're willing to come, I can keep you safe from her. But we have to go now, as quick as we can."

She laughs, just a short, sharp chuckle. "I can handle a horse, you know."

"Not this horse."

I see in her eyes the slow realization of what I am saying.

"A horse…" she says.

I nod. The woman returns with the requested supplies. Fairlight immediately pulls the bag over her shoulder as she speaks to her. "Bring the others behind us," she says. "Be careful. The two of us will go on ahead and light a beacon fire as soon as we can. The two of us will go and see about this boy. Be careful, but come as soon as you can. You have time to arrive before nightfall."

We approach Mare. I issue small comforting noises to her

as we approach. She balks at the sight of Fairlight, baring her teeth and flattening her tattered ears against her head.

"Dear god, what's the matter with her?" Fairlight asks. "She's like them, isn't she? She's turned like the zombies."

"Yeah."

Fairlight tucked her bag under her arm, securing the strap across her chest. "What do you call her?"

"Mare. Her name is Mare."

"It suits her I suppose."

I manage to keep her calm enough to allow me to swing up onto her back. I extend my hand to lift Fairlight's slight form onto Mare's back. She eyed the exposed muscle on the neck and flanks of the creature.

"She won't hurt you," I say, feeling strangely defensive at her hesitation. She takes my hand and pulls up onto the horse behind me, settling in as well as she can.

It feels strange, the connection between me and this horse. I don't understand it, but it serves useful. I sense her hunger, her discomfort at Fairlight's presence. But she allows us to ride her, speeding up when I spur her forward.

Ezekiel waits at the gate when we arrive. Fairlight seems all too eager to slide off the horse and cross the threshold into the safety of the farm. Once inside, he leads us to Thorn, lying on the blanket next to the fire pit.

"I managed to get the bleeding slowed down," Ezekiel says. "But we don't have anything to prevent infection."

"That's my department," Fairlight says as she approaches. "Is the bullet still inside?"

"I think so. Ash?"

I pace back and forth, running my fingers through my hair.

"I know that look," he says. "What are you thinking?"

I don't answer right away, casting my gaze to the

surrounding countryside, the forest's edge, the weed tangled garden, with the house now an empty shell of what was once a haven filled with hope and laughter.

"Ash?" he says once more.

I turn to meet his gaze, finally feeling a glimpse of understanding to his constant anger. "I'm going back," I say.

"Oh, come on, Ash. You can't--"

"She won't stop. She'll never stop. All of this is her fault. She'll just keep going until she's destroyed everything. It's her fault the world is like this. It's her fault I'm like this, that your parents are dead."

"Ash--"

"I have to end this, Eze. I have to find her and one way or another, I have to end it."

He nods. "Okay. Yeah. I get it. Come on."

"Where are we going?"

"You'll need weapons," he says. "That's the one thing I can help you with."

He pulls open the door to the warehouse, revealing the hidden vehicles, stores of food, and, perhaps most important, the cache of weapons where Eden had kept my crossbow when I first arrived here. That felt like ages ago.

The sunlight streams through the door, illuminating the space, a plethora of weaponry. Blades, arrows, slings, an array of guns in various sizes. The collection takes my breath away.

"How do you have all this?" I ask.

"Oh, Mom and Dad started collecting weapons long before the Fall," he replies. "They knew things would go south. Wanted to be prepared."

"Wow..." I exhale.

"I understand that you don't have a preference for guns,

but you are welcome to anything you can take, anything you might need. I'll let you browse. Take your time." He exits the warehouse, leaving me alone with the weapons cache.

My first order of business is to find compatible bolts for the crossbow. Ezekiel is right about my aversion to guns. One might as well hold up a target with a sign reading, "Eat Me Zombies."

I locate three sheaths worth of arrows on the bottom shelf, just underneath a drawer full of smoke bombs. Two of these I tuck into the front pocket of my backpack.

Perusing the shelves, I add a Bowie knife to each hip and a belt of throwing stars across my torso. The added weight actually feels good. I slip a couple of switchblades into my boots and step out of the enclosure.

"You got it?" Ezekiel asks.

"Yeah, I think so."

"I'd say." He gives me a once over, taking in my new inventory. "We should stop and fill our water canisters before you head out."

We follow along the tree line back toward the spring. Once I fill mine, he steps up and tops off his canister as well. From here I can see, through the trees, Fairlight tending to Thorn. Alma crouches next to her at the ready for any needed assistance.

"He'll be alright," Ezekiel says, following my gaze.

"What?"

"It's obvious you care about him."

"I mean, I don't--"

"No, it's okay," he says. "We have to take what we can get. I don't think it hit anything vital and Fairlight's got the bleeding under control. He'll be okay."

All I can do is exhale. I hadn't realized how shallow I had been breathing.

"Um, Ash? I think you've got company." He gestures

toward the edge of the gate.

I follow his gaze, spotting a familiar figure at the far end of the fence. Even from here I can clearly make out the yellow dress and matted hair. She stands completely still, staring towards us.

A fury of emotion boils up within me. Carrying this secret had worn on me, this burden which I kept from everyone. The knowledge of what I could do crept upon me, awakening a fury which only the truth would vanquish.

"I know that look," Ezekiel says, watching my expression. "I'd go with you, if I thought you'd let me."

I turn my gaze toward him. With some small dawning of surprise, I realize we have become friends. Somehow, over the course of the past few months, a tentative respect grew up between us where once stood animosity.

Somehow, some way, this knowledge now existed that either one of us would stand and fight alongside the other. Without question or hesitation. When had that changed?

"I know you would," I say.

I cross the path circling away from the firepit. I offer a quick wave to the women and head toward the gate. I've got a lot of ground to cover before daylight ends.

Eleven

I walk away from the farm, leading the horse with the bridle, Penny shuffling along on my left.

Her presence remains a mystery. I did not call to her or beckon in any way. She's just here. And this horse, it only makes sense she eats flesh, just like the others, but still. I find her bloodstained muzzle a bit unnerving.

We keep to the road, moving slowly. Mare ambles along, her head bobbing with each step. As we go, I realize the mental connection between us feels stronger now that the distractions of the farm are no longer present.

And just like that, the same familiar feeling creeps up on me. The further away we get, the more comfortable I feel with my motley companions. Perhaps I am more like them after all.
We arrive at the same place in the road where the horde had found that deer. I wouldn't have noticed, except that Penny stops dead in her tracks.

"What is it?" I ask, but she just stands there, staring at me the same way she always does.

I step toward her. As I do, she takes a step to the left. Her movements remind me of that one zombie in the forest who mirrored my movements. I test her by taking another step toward the forest's edge.

She does not mirror my actions like the other one had done. Rather, she transposes my steps. For every step I take forward, she moves one to the side.

Mare exhales in a low moan, shuffling one foot and tossing her head. I remember what happened when I had placed my hand on her muzzle the first time we met.

Penny stands about an arm's length away from me. I lift

my hand, painfully aware of the short distance between her exposed teeth and my bare forearm. Let's just hope this works. I lift my hand ever so carefully, placing my fingertips against her forehead.

Her skin feels cool to the touch, dry and papery. It gives slightly at my touch. Most importantly, though, my theory is correct.

The skin-to-skin contact strengthens the connection between us. Until now I had assumed her actions were because of my influence, that whatever will they had left consisted of nothing more than insatiable hunger, but this... This feels different.

I remove my hand and take a step back, a small tendril of fear stirring within me.

"What do you want, Penny?"

She takes another step.

"Do you... Do you want me to follow you?" I ask. I step forward, copying the step she has just taken. She walks forward a few more feet, turning to look at me again with those glazed, white eyes.

"Alright then." I keep after her.

Behind me, Mare takes a few steps to stay with us. We make our way through the forest with Penny leading the way. Finding the path of least resistance, she makes her way through the forest, slinking between tree trunks and fallen vines. I do my best to find my way over the uneven ground, which seems to have no effect on her.

"I wonder..." I say, taking a step back and placing my hand on Mare's flank.

Penny pauses, turning to look at me again. I'll never get used to that gaze. The horse comes to a stop and I pull myself up onto her back.

"Maybe your footing will be better than mine," I murmur. "Okay, let's go."

We resume our trek. I lean forward to avoid the branches and brambles around us. Penny moves with a bizarre sure-footedness which I have never seen with her kind.

Finally, we arrive at our destination. I recognize the edge of the quarry from my previous encounter here. Below us, hundreds of zombies fill the air with the stench of the undead.

"What's your game, Penny?" I ask.

She continues to ignore me, cresting the edge and stumbling down the rocky edge, joining with the group. I do my best to keep my eyes on her to track her path.

To my surprise she stops in the dead center of the horde. The others shuffle around her, oblivious to her presence. She stops and turns toward me, dead white eyes raised to meet my gaze.

"Intention," I mutter. "She's doing this stuff on purpose. What does that mean?"

Mare's low whinny is the only response, a ghostly, haunted sound. I reach down and pat her flank, careful not to touch her exposed muscle.

"What do you think, Mare? Should we go ahead and make camp here?" It feels strange setting up this close to them, but I need to be where I can observe them for now. I slide off the side of the horse, finding my footing. The rumble in my stomach reminds me that my needs are more immediate than those of my traveling companions.

I gather enough wood to start a small fire. The grove of trees creates a smooth parcel of land, covered over by branches, enough to serve as a makeshift shelter.

One of the trees forms a large Y in its branches where I stash my backpack for now. Considering my current security detail, I don't imagine they are in any danger of theft. I walk over to Mare and pat her flank.

"I'll be back in a little bit," I say. "I'll bring you something to eat, okay?"

She tosses her head in response.

A few hours later, a pheasant happily roasts over the fire in front of me. I had caught three, the other two being currently grazed on by Mare, making noisy work of the carcasses, gnashing her teeth on the meat and bones.

I pull mine from the fire, setting it on the bed of leaves to cool. The sun hovers far too close to the horizon for me to get much else done today.

That's okay. I've found my bearings, but tomorrow I have a feeling I'll need a good night of rest.

I pluck at the food, knowing I need to replenish but not having much of an appetite. The idea of confronting Dr. Donovan does not appeal to me, but I know it is my only recourse. I have to give her a chance, at least.

To... to what? Explain herself? Give all of it up and come back to SeaHaven with the rest of us? That's a long shot.
I wrap up the rest of the bird and tuck it in the branches of the tree. The night air will cool it enough for me to eat cold in the morning. Stretching out on the ground, I tuck my arm behind my head, letting my gaze wander across the tableau of stars.

Already, I had grown accustomed to the moans and shuffling coming from the horde on the other side of the canyon's edge, now nothing more than white noise. Just as I lay down, I sense the change.

The chaotic mumble grows suddenly quiet, diminished. I roll over enough to take in the view beyond the edge. The zombies below stand in rows, perfectly symmetrical and shoulder to shoulder.

"What the hell..." I mutter.

Splitting pain erupts within my head, erasing all possibility of further thought. I cry out, clutching at my head, my knees curled up against my stomach. Even the dim night feels too bright, piercing into my eyes and forcing them shut.

I don't know how much time passes before the pain subsides. Could be seconds. Could be minutes. I let it happen, doing my best to detach myself from it.

Finally, I manage to open my eyes. They are walking in step with one another, just like a large, well-trained army, marching forward. I see Penny in the midst of them in perfect lockstep, stiff and jolting.

Through squinted eyes, I follow the edge of the canyon, trying to ascertain where they are going. Up ahead is a curve, a bend in the path where the forerunners of the horde have already vanished.

I have just enough strength to crawl along the edge of the ravine, trying to find a path down to try and follow them. The pain in my head overwhelms my ability to guess where they are going.

I try, but the pain only intensifies, forcing me to let go. I'm just glad I have some distance from camp before I get sick. I make my way back to the tree, lying still in the grass. Keeping still helps just a bit, willing myself against the oncoming disorientation. Closing my eyes against the starlight. The passage of time becomes meaningless.

Eventually, I fall asleep.

When morning comes, I find them all there, the undead wandering about the bottom of the ravine as if they had been there the whole night. My headache is gone, but I feel groggy, and my muscles feel sore. I stand slowly, making my way toward the tree where I had stored the food the night before.

The food helps. Mare roams about, nibbling here and there on the remains of the bloody pheasants from the previous day. She does not wander far, but she keeps pawing at the ground, her ears flicking, spraying tiny globules rot into her mane.

"What is it? What's bothering you, Mare?"

I follow her gaze toward the horizon. A dust storm appears to be churning in the distance. Nothing to worry about. It could just be a weather anomaly.

"Is that what's bothering you?" I stroke her flank. She feels quite agitated, more so than I have felt before from her. An image drifts into my mind, an image which offers a horrifying clarity.

Horses. The dust kicking up in the distance is a herd of wild horses running free. Pure, natural, wild horses. She feels them, longing to run alongside them.

"You're still in there, aren't you girl?" I place my hand flat against her flank, absorbing as much of our connection as possible.

Deep within her, I sense the longing for grass and hay, a friendly hand with a sugar cube inside. She envies their freedom, their wholeness.

She whinnies, frightened and lonely. Her sadness pours into me. I let go, stepping away. She trots away from the camp, heading toward the wild horses, circling back and pawing at the ground.

I sit down at the edge of the ravine, letting my feet swing beneath me. The creatures wander, bumping into each other, mindless, still continuing to ignore one another.

I find Penny out there in the middle. Is she different, I wonder? What makes her seek me out the way she does? Is she still in there the way Mare seems to be? Could it be that some kind of conscience remains buried inside her? The thought makes me queasy.

I stand up and brush my hands across my legs. It's time to find the doctor. I need answers.

I pick up my belongings, covering the campfire with dirt, scattering the remaining ashes. Just as I finish up, Mare returns. The holes in her coat have expanded, large patches of flesh falling away around her legs. I see glimpses of pale bones between tattered muscles. I wonder how much time she has before I can't ride her anymore, before she falls apart.

"Do you want to come along, Mare?" I murmur.

Carefully, I roll my backpack across her shoulders as usual, but she arches her back, tossing it off onto the ground.

"Not up for it, right now. I see. That's alright, then. It's probably better I do this one on my own." Her muzzle against my palm feels cold and wrinkled, like a rotten peach.

I wonder if I will see her again, after I leave this time. Reaching up, I unclasp the bridle, opting to let her roam as she sees fit. She deserves to finish out her days as she chooses, if this can even be considered a life.

As I reach up my hand brushes against the area beneath her ear. I feel a hard ridge of flesh along the edge of her jawbone.

"What's this?"

She lets me examine the area. It appears scarred over in such a way that I think it must have happened before she turned. The fur had long since fallen out, leaving an exposed patch. I press my fingertips along the edge of the bone, discovering a small knot just underneath her skin.

"What *is* this?" I say again.

Taking out my knife, I slide it along the flesh beneath the scar, knowing this will not hurt her. She does not flinch as I perform the impromptu surgery.

Just as I suspected, an implant of some kind reveals itself beneath her skin. I pull it out without much trouble, covered in greenish black ichor, a metallic disk about the size of the pad of my thumb.

"Wait," I mutter. I rub the item across the ground, in an attempt to clear it of the viscous liquid. I reach into my backpack, fingers searching the small outer pocket until I touch upon the item, the disc I had pulled from the zombie. They are nearly identical.

"Oh, my god…" I whisper. "What has she done to you?" I feel the change in her energy with my hand against her muzzle. She feels… calm, less afraid. I, on the other hand, feel disjointed, as if I have a box of puzzle pieces I can't figure out how to put together.

I pull my pack over one shoulder and hitch my crossbow snug against the small of my back. I double check my knife belt and water supply.

It is time to go.

I bid her a final farewell, placing my forehead against hers, hoping perhaps to feel some of the peace she now possesses.

"Take care of yourself," I whisper. "Go now. Go be a horse for a little while longer."

I turn and head toward the road. The landscape looks familiar within minutes. The last time I traveled this way, we were all still here. Thorn, Rose, Alma, Travis… I remember how much we had wanted to stay away from the zombies, to keep out of their way.

Once upon a time, we called them the enemy. Today, by some twist of fate, they had become my ally.

I don't see any zombies as I go. Perhaps they all had been corralled into the ravine where I'd left them. In the distance, I finally see the compound against the horizon.

Time to press on, I decide. Another few hours, at most. I've got plenty of daylight. Best to get this over with.I continue forward, keeping the building in sight.

Twelve

Getting inside the compound could prove to be a bit of a challenge, as the last time I did so I was unconscious. I take the only path I know, around the edge of the horse field, making my way toward the stables.

I had not recognized the space due to the angle, but once I pass by the stable yard, I see the break in the wall, now an empty chasm leading straight into the compound.

Now the easiest way in, this place used to be teeming with zombies. Donovan called it the moat, a strip of land fenced and filled with zombies to keep out the danger, and to keep everyone else inside.

I make no effort to remain stealthy as I climb over the broken concrete. Pieces shift and tumble, but I make my way over and into the hallway.

Immediately, I find myself faced with a clutch of five zombies, scattered across the hallway. The sounds of my actions drew their attention, skeletal cheeks and sunken eyes peering as they turn towards me.

"Of course," I mutter, reaching for my knife. "What's a family reunion without a handful of zombies?"

The one closest to me, once upon a time a middle-aged woman with long brown hair, runs towards me in quick herky-jerky steps. Fast, like the others, teeth gnashing without purpose.

My blade lands in the side of her neck, sending a tendril of gelatinous blood spewing across my arm. She collapses once I draw the blade through her neck and across her brain stem.

"Sorry, sister," I say to her fallen corpse. "You were in my way."

The next one comes at me straight on. The very fact they

are attacking me confirms she is controlling them somehow.

The knife handle slips in my hand, covered in viscous blood. I lose purchase for a moment, holding him back with my forearm against his collar bone.

His rotted face is inches from mine, snapping into the air. I turn away, grimacing against the odor of decay blooming from his mouth.

Another comes in behind me, arms grasping me with surprising strength. I stretch my other arm behind me, knife still in hand but slipping against my fingers every time I try to get a decent grip on it.

Turning by body I manage to keep them each at arm's length, one hand pressed on each of their bony chests. There is only one way out.

I drop to my knees and scurry out from between their legs, turning onto my backside and scooting as far as I can down the narrow hallway. The two of them fall into a tangled mass, unable to follow my trajectory.

I flip my crossbow around and fire off one bolt, piercing both of their heads.

"Not bad," I mutter. "Three down. Two to go."

But the remaining two don't attack. By some unseen signal, they stand at attention.

My head aches. My desire to find Donovan increases to a fever pitch. I lean against the stock of the crossbow, pulling myself to my feet.

"Where are you!" I call out, my voice cracking.

"Now, now. There's no reason to shout, Ashley." Her voice echoes from the com speakers embedded into the walls. "You've done so well. It's so good to see you."

So, she can see me. Okay, that's good to know. But where is she, hidden away in the depths of her castle?

I remember the evening announcement for curfew during my time here before, emanating from these same speakers set all over the campus. This compound had teemed with life then, families, children. Now the empty hallway stretched before me like a cavernous tomb.

"Keep walking," she says. "I'll guide you."

"Are you sure you want me to be in the same room with you?" I call back, my voice echoing against the metallic walls.

"Just follow my instructions for now. We'll have to save the conversation for when we are face to face. Something I greatly look forward to. I only hope you feel the same." Her disembodied voice sounds strange through the com system, somehow even more sinister than I remember.

"I can assure you, I don't," I mutter under my breath.

"Keep walking forward to the end of the hall," she says. "Don't worry. The creatures won't bother you anymore. Once you get to the end, turn left. There you'll find a door leading to the stairs. I would take you to the elevators, but unfortunately, they stopped working when the compound switched to auxiliary power. A necessary safety measure should there be a breech."

I did my best to ignore the hidden meaning, the twist in her voice as she spoke these words. The breech, of course, meaning the time I drove a truck through the library wall for the dual purpose of getting everyone out, and allowing in the immeasurable number of flesh-eating zombies swarming the outer walls of the compound.

She leads me up two flights of stairs to another door and into another hallway. Each time I pass through one, I stop and take the time to pull them shut behind me, minimizing the sound of the door closing. Old habits die hard, I guess.

Finally, I arrive at one of the doors at the end of the hallway. I recognize the position of the building, that this room sits at the edge of the compound.

The balcony where I had seen her would no doubt be connected on the other side. With a steady hand, I reach forward, turning the handle and opening the door.

"Hello, my prodigal child," she says as she turns toward me. "I've been expecting you."

"Doctor," I reply.

She lights up, clapping her hands in some apparent delight. At what, I don't know. Her eyes flash with a wildness, her hair unkempt around her face. "Come and see. Let me show you, what you and I have done."

You and I?

She places one hand over a large dial, turning and adjusting, while her other hand flies over the number pad, punching in some unknown code. The panel lights up, flashing in a sequence.

I step forward enough to bring the horde below us into view. Just as they had done in the ravine, they lined up, triggered by some signal, shoulder to shoulder, at attention, with upturned, ghoulish faces, rows of sentries awaiting their orders.
Orders from her.

"You… You've created an army of them."

"Yes, I have. Aren't they beautiful…?"

"But what are you going to do with them?" I say with growing trepidation.

"No, dear. What are *we* going to do with them."

"It doesn't have to be this way," I say in a desperate attempt to reach her.

"Yes, Ash. It does."

"Come back with me," I say. "Come back with me to SeaHaven. You'll see, there are people there, a community. We can start over. You don't have to do this."

"Oh, Ash," she says, her face resting into that simpering falsity of niceness. "It's too late for that. I had truly hoped you would join me willingly."

"Why would I do that?" I ask.

"Child, you've lived so long in this cruel world, growing up without a mother's love. It's not too late, you know."

"You're not my mother, and anything you gave me was nothing like a mother's love. You killed my mother!"

"If we had known of her state when she came to us. Putting you in danger like that."

"You would have done it anyway! You wouldn't have changed a thing! Infecting her the way you did... It's *your* fault I'm like this! Not hers!"

She responds with a disappointing shake of her head, reaching over to the console. Immediately, I fall to the ground, an invisible pressure rendering me incapacitated. I clasp at my head, fingers digging into my skull.

"You know," she says, "if you give in, it won't hurt so much."

"I'll never give in..."

"If you just listen, darling girl. Just stop and listen to what it is that you want, what you truly want, then you'll begin to understand."

I pull myself into a ball, cringing against the pain, clutching my arms around my knees. What I want is for the pain to end.

I barely focus on her nonsensical stream of words. Somewhere in the back of my mind, tumblers turn, the smallest whisper of an answer, but I cannot grasp its meaning.

Another moment, and it is gone.

"What do you want from me?" I say in a voice heavy with pain.

109

She leans down next to me. "It is not what I want from you, Ash. It is what you want."

"And what is it, exactly, that *I* want?"

"Your whole life you have denied yourself one thing. The part of you that you are most ashamed of, which you have kept hidden, even from yourself. The part of you which is like them. You have kept it hidden for so long. You want to let it go, let that part of yourself free. You want nothing more than to be who you truly are, Ash."

"I can't," I reply. "I won't. I don't want to be a monster."

"No, of course not my darling!" she purrs. "Not a monster at all. You are my own beautiful child, the first of many. And now you are home, and we can make this all right again."

"No…"

"Let me ask you a question, Ash."

"Please, just make it stop…"

She stands, moving toward the console once more. "Did you find it difficult to make your way back here?"

"What are you talking about?"

"The journey here to the compound, was it particularly difficult?"

"Why do you…"

"Did you come here because you chose to?"

"Of course I did. Why else would I…" All of a sudden, the tumblers fall into place. I did not come here of my own accord. She drew me in, just as she had the others.

"Don't you see?" she says. "I've done all of this to find you. You are the key to making this work. I created the frequency for you. All the rest was just a happy accident."

"But I won't do it," I reply between clenched teeth. "I won't do what you want me to do."

She smiled, simpering. "Such a sweet girl. You see, when

you left us this last time, I felt as if I had lost you all over again, just like when you were a child. I knew I had to find a way to make you come back to me. Luckily, one of my most loyal scientists helped me find a way."

"I came here to end this!"

"No." She reaches over to the console, placing one trembling finger on the dial. With just a touch, the sensation in my head rises another level, pressure throbbing through my ears. "You came here because I called you. You and I, mother and daughter, side by side, we can rebuild this world. A world which I have created and you will inherit. A new humanity. Better, stronger. Don't you see?"

"You've gone mad," I whisper.

She turns the dial another notch. The pain consumes me, knocking me to my knees, coursing through me. Fire. Thunder. My head squeezed from all sides.

I find myself unable to cry out against it. Nothing more than a whimper escapes my lips.

"I want you to know, I take no joy in seeing you like this," she says. "But it is a vital part of your purpose, Ash. This is a good pain, like childbirth."

"What?" I manage to croak.

"The pain will subside after a few moments. Come. Let's get you to your room. You've been through a lot today. We'll start again tomorrow. In the meantime, you need your rest."

She takes my arm, steadying me to my feet and guiding me forward. Begrudgingly, I lean against her, not quite trusting my feet.

We walk along the hallway leading toward my room, still fully intact, just as I had left it. The pink bedding and pastel shelves, loaded with ridiculous toys.

This is all too much. I cannot fight her. The pain in my

head   feels   far   too   great.

She leads me through the door, guiding me to lie down on the bed before undressing me with clinical care. The sheets feel cool against my fatigued body as she pulls them up to my shoulders. I hear her move about the room, and then, a moment later, she places a hot dry cloth over my closed eyes and forehead. The sensation immediately offers relief to my aching head.

"Good night, Ashley," she whispers, placing the back of her fingers gently against my cheek. "Rest now. I'll come and fetch you in the morning. I'm sure you'll be hungry from the activation."

I hate her. I can't move my arms or legs, and my body sinks into the coolness of the sheets. I hate that she has somehow gained the upper hand.

Swimming with confusion, my mind gives up. The lights dim and she leaves the room, pausing for only a moment before pulling the door shut behind her.

Thirteen

The next morning, I find my head feels much better. I can't say as much for my mood.

I recall a dream of SeaHaven, of hot food and laughter. Penny was there, her weird, rotten self, just standing there the way she always does, staring at me. She lifts her hands, reaching for me.

Everyone around us appears oblivious to her presence. The dream drifted away to the view of the sunlight sparkling through the window.

Managing to get up on my feet, I cross the room, trying the door. To my surprise it opens. How far can I get before she tries to stop me, I wonder?

Grabbing my pack and crossbow, I make my way down the hallway with every intention of just leaving. She can't make me stay.

I don't see Dr. Donovan anywhere and I don't go looking for her. Perhaps she is watching me from some room deep in the compound, watching me run from one screen to the other. No matter. The doctor is the least of my concerns.

I see no one until I reach the fence outside, running alongside the now vacant paddock. I spot the farmhand at the far side, absently pushing a wheelbarrow.

If he looked up, he would see me, plain as day. Only about ten feet separates me from the coverage of the forest. I could make a run for it, but I'd risk discovery.

Crouching below the edge of the rock wall, my mind twists at how to escape. It's so close. Glancing back, I see the man disappear behind the barn doors.

I spring forward, sprinting for the tree line. Within

minutes, I slip into the shadows, only pausing long enough to glance back.

At the corner of the barn, the farmhand stands, looking directly toward where I had just been hiding. I steel myself for the inevitable call of warning, but it never comes. He just stands there, perfectly still, a bemused, nearly satisfied look on his face.

Had he seen me? Even more peculiar, had he let me go? I don't take the time to dwell on it.

My feet catch against the roots and rocks, forcing me to slow down. But I continue forward, willing myself to keep moving.

The sun creeps towards its apex and the rumbling in my stomach reminds me that I need to find something to eat. I have plenty of arrows, so I could stake out in a tree somewhere if I wanted to. The idea of hunting does not appeal to me in any way though.

A wave of disorientation washes over me. I steady myself against the nearest tree. I need to keep moving, but I've lost my sense of direction. Perhaps I need food more than I realized. I move forward, slower this time, one foot in front of the other.

Penny arrives in front of me, shuffling towards me through the trees. Her bright yellow dress stands out between the shadows.

I realize I have retraced my steps back to the ravine without even thinking about it. How long have I been walking? Her hand stretches out to me, beckoning with her staring, dead eyes.

I reach out and take her hand. My head swims. I can't focus. Hunger overwhelms my senses. Penny guides me along to the edge of the ravine. I lose my footing, but manage to control my fall, sliding through the falling rocks until we reach the bottom.

I stand, brushing off my legs, but my hands and arms feel thick, clumsy. I need water. I need to eat.

Of course, the gathering horde, they don't touch me. Only Penny, who reaches for my hand once more. She pulls me along the ravine floor, dodging between the others until we arrive at our destination.

She leads me to the edge of the ravine, and in the wall facing us a small trickle of water emerges from the side, caught in a crevasse before tumbling down the rock face.

I kneel and scoop handfuls of the water to my mouth. Despite tasting a bit gamey, it feels cool against my throat. I try not to think about the microscopic beings which may live within. I drink for several minutes, ignoring the movements of the creatures surrounding me.

With my thirst sated, I turn toward Penny. She stares blankly ahead towards where the others move, gathering around something a short distance away. Hunched over some newly dead animal like a bunch of vultures. A coyote, by the sound of the pack howling in the surrounding forest above us and the silver paws, the only recognizable parts of the bloody carcass, visible at the edge of the tableau.

The zombies drag around the body, gnawing at the meat. Strings of flesh, ripped and shredded, hang from their bloody teeth.

The copper aroma teases my hunger, strangely tantalizing to my empty stomach. Penny turns, beckoning to me with her dead eyes.

"I can't eat this kind of food," I say. My mouth feels heavy, my tongue leaden.

Turning back to the water, in hopes to satiate my growing hunger, I catch sight of my reflection in the still water. My skin appears pale, almost green. Perhaps nothing more than an illusion caused by the traces of algae within the water, I think.

But my eyes betray the truth of it. They appear milky and pale, vacant. With my hair matted with dirt and leaves, my lips cracked and pale, I realize what I look like.
I look like them.

"What has she done to me?" I whisper. The words come out as a garbled, incoherent growl.

Penny appears next to me, peering into the water as if curious. She places her rotting hand next to mine, resting on the edge of the basin.

Side by side, I see just how similar we have become, she and I. The only difference between us appears to be the decay around her fingernails. Mine have gone pale blue, hers dark gray. The thin, paper-like flesh remaining on her skeletal hands bears the same pale color as my own.

I give up fighting, at least just for the moment. Penny wants me to follow her, a strange act of empathy with my hunger.
She feels the same need. She seems to be… living somehow. Different than before. She died once, a violent, unexpected, unfair death, and she turned into this.

How have I become like her?

I glance over to the prone beast lying on the ground, nearly eviscerated by the few remaining zombies. Between them, I spot the skin peeled back, exposing the musculature of the dead coyote. The blood and flesh call to me. I move forward, shuffling on my knees and nudging my way into the horde.

Hesitating only a moment, I plunge my hands into the flesh, pulling out shreds of bloody muscle, scooping them into my mouth.

The taste immediately calms me. I no longer care or have the capacity to think about my actions, devouring… bite after bite, quenching my hunger.

Every day of my life, this feeling has been with me. Unrecognized but unwavering, satisfied only by this raw, naked flesh. We eat until there is nothing left.

I have become one of them.

I have become the undead.

Fourteen

My stomach feels tight and full. For the first time in a long time, I feel sated.

I crawl a few feet away from the carcass, my hands and face sticky with blood. The sight of it does not bother me like it might have in previous days. Now, I want nothing, except to sleep. Apparently, I am not the only one.

The others have curled up on the ground, a macabre nest, each resting on the other, fully satiated. Yes. I spot a corner of the clowder, enough room for me.

My limbs feel heavy. I cannot stand. On hands and knees, I make my way toward them, craving the warmth of their presence.

Penny's head rests against the leg of another, her arms and legs drawn up to her chest, the very picture of a sleeping child. I mirror her actions, resting my head against her leg before giving myself over to the sleep threatening to consume me. Perhaps tomorrow I will think on this, but tonight I am satisfied.

My eyes flicker toward the starlit sky, sparkling gemstones against the void. We drift into slumber. I welcome the embrace of the horde.

Somehow, Donovan has won, I realize, with a smile drifting across my face. I don't fight it. I welcome it.

Let her win.

As long as I have a full stomach and a place to rest after. This is all I want, all I need. Nothing else matters. Not anymore.

I don't remember waking. I don't remember standing or moving in any particular direction. The only awareness I have is walking.

One step. Another step. Another. Another.

Shoulder to shoulder, we move as one. The cold flesh of the others presses against me from all sides. It comforts me.

I am them.

They are me.

Our hunger grows and we walk. Through the ravine. Toward the forest.

There is sustenance in the forest. The living. A mother deer and her fawn, vibrant and pulsing with fresh, blooded meat. Waiting for us to consume them.

We walk.

Hunger consumes us. Growing painful. I crave relief.

We move through the trees, moving apart and together again. One step. Another. Another. Skin scrapes against the rough bark. Keep moving forward. Find something to eat.

We find the deer, curled up in a grassy grove, tucked into the cavern created beneath the roots of a large tree, with her spotted fawn nestled at her belly. They never even have a chance. The first ones to reach them fall on them mercilessly. Even before I reach the grove, I smell the blood.

Enticing. Calling to me.

They kill her quickly. And the fawn. Nothing more than swash of a bloody carcass by the time I reach them.

We descend, consuming with abandon. Tearing flesh,hot blood pours over my lips and teeth, warming my tongue, my throat, my stomach.

Again, we sleep. Crawling into the corners of the forest, tucked away in relative safety of our numbers. Arms and legs piled together. Rotted flesh, fighting against the inevitable decay of passing time.

Again, we walk. Rising to find the nearest living. Further into the forest we move. Step after step. This time, a family of turtles falls prey to our hunt.

Everything. Even the shells, crunched up between skeletal teeth.

One of our kind gets stuck in the water. Trapped at an angle, his feet caught in the clay. We walk onward, uncaring about those fallen. We move as one unit, turning towards the food, consuming, and then moving on.

Days pass.

We come to a building, a distant outcropping at first. My words have long since left me. But the meaning of what I see still sneaks through the recesses of my mind.

Warehouse.

The others feel the presence of sustenance inside, the living. Just one. I don't feel the same familiar pull as I would with a deer or wolf carcass like we find in the forests, but the others continue to move forward, drawn by hunger.

I can only follow. They've been doing this longer than I have. They must know something I don't. We close in on it, a large edifice at the edge of an abandoned city.

Like them, I sense something inside the building, a living thing, moving, breathing, pulsating. But I am not compelled towards it. A buried thread of curiosity compels me onward, still one of the horde.

The explosions go nearly unnoticed. A zombie falls. The others continue onward, falling and shuffling over, around, toward the prey. Closer to me, another zombie falls, his head snapping back as dead blood sprays from the back of his head, before he crumbles to the ground.

I hear nothing, but clarity blooms within me. Someone is shooting at us. My life might be in danger. How can that be? These thoughts don't connect. Disembodied. Drifting across my conscience.

Another zombie falls, blocking my path. The others around me stumble, building an obstruction of tangled body parts, still reaching, struggling forward. The weight of our horde presses forward. I step to the side, avoiding the fallen ones.

Perhaps this movement out of the shuffling march of the others jogs my awareness, perhaps the proximity of another human, I don't know, but something shifts. The tiniest change inside me, I look up.

She is there.

A woman stands on the roof of the building. She holds a gun. A large gun with a sleek metal barrel, tucked into her arms, her eye lowered to the sights.

She fires. The recoil kicks into her shoulder, but her feet planted in a wide stance don't move. She picks them off, one by one.

Does she see me? The idea that she could shoot me only feels like some distant annoyance. I need to get her attention somehow.

Just as soon as the thought drifts across my mind, it is gone. I am back to being one with the horde, nothing more than a creature surrounded by creatures, seeking, yearning, devouring.

This woman, she is our prey. Nothing more.

The shooting pain in my upper arm knocks me back, tumbling into the row of zombies behind me. As usual, they ignore my presence, moving around me blindly.

I look up. The woman peers down at me with the gun lowered to her side, her expression clouded. She backs away, disappearing from view.

I push through the horde. The front edge has already met the side of the building and they press forward. I have seen this before.

Get enough zombies in a horde and they can take down a

building. Maybe not one this size, but I've seen how strong they can be. I keep pushing forward, elbowing through them to try and get to the front.

The pain in my arm pushes through, a final grasp on my humanity. I clutch my right hand across the wound on my left arm, blood seeping through my fingers.

My head feels swimmy. This time I know it is not from lack of food. A flickering light gains my attention, shining from the far corner of the building.

Flash.

Flash.

Then nothing. And again.

Flash.

Flash.

None of them seem to notice. I push to the side, still clutching at my bleeding arm, shoving my way through before I get caught up in the pressing throng of bodies.

Somehow my awareness shifts to the stifling odor of decaying flesh. How did I not notice this before? I struggle to keep breathing steady. At last, I push through.

I see the woman standing on a platform, some kind of lift protruding from the outer wall. She gestures to me, waving her hand over her head.

I spot the mirror in her hand, sunlight glinting off the surface. I return the wave with my uninjured arm. She leans down, crouching onto her knees and throws a rope over the edge of the platform.

How am I going to climb that with one arm, I wonder? But I get there, and I grab hold, planting my feet on the knot at the base. The immediate tension signals that I don't have to worry about climbing. She pulls me up, as close to the metal edge as possible, and helps me onto the surface.

"You bit?" she asks in a thick, raspy southern accent.

"No, I'm not bit."

"Sorry I winged ya," she says. "How the hell'd you do that anyhow?"

"Do what?" I reply.

"Come on. Let's get inside. Getcha cleaned up. We got plenty a time to chat."

I follow her in. The opening doesn't appear to be a door or a window. Just some kind of square hole in the middle of the wall. Up on this level, I spot about six more of them down the length of the building.

"What is this place?" I ask.

She walks over to a collection of couches placed in a circle. In the center sits a small burner, with a pan of thick bubbling liquid in the middle.

It smells like... food.

Actual food, not the raw meat I had been consuming for the past... how long had I been out there? "Well, it used to be a distributing warehouse. Now," she gestures for me to have a seat, "it's my own home sweet home."

Collecting supplies from a shelf, she approaches me. First, she hands me a bottle of water. I feel disoriented, so I don't argue when she begins to tend to my arm. She pours a clear, strong smelling liquid over the wound, sending a sharp pain ricocheting through me. I suck in my breath, tensing at the unexpected sensation.

"Sorry about that." She lifts my arm, placing a white gauze over it and wrapping a white bandage around my bicep.

"This ought to do ya."

As she completes the task, I take a look around us. This corner appears cozy and homey. Pieces of newspaper strewn about, a collection of paperback books piled in a disheveled stack next to the overstuffed chair. They all looked quite dog-eared and well read.

On the other side, a mountain of bottled water, most of it still wrapped in plastic, covers the adjacent wall.

But on beyond, in the dim shadows, I can see just how large of a building this is. Rows upon rows of shelves, stretching further than I can make out, towering toward the ceiling. I cannot even see the back wall.

"Forgive me for sayin', but you look a right mess. You want to get cleaned up? I was just about to have a bite, but it will keep long enough. Come on. I'll show you the shower."

I follow her, downing the water she had given me. Perhaps I was more thirsty than I realized. She leads me to another open area, a patio of sorts, but the railing had been built up with wooden fencing, creating a closed-off space open to the sky. The far corner contains a hanging contraption, a series of rubber tubing connected to a rain barrel.

"Here you go," she says. "If you pull here, the water comes out here. It'll be a mite cold, but there's not much else we can do about that. I'll put you out a change of clothes."

"You have clothes?"

"Honey, I got just about everything in here." She shrugs, her lined face falling into a tragic expression for a brief moment."Just about."

With that, she leaves me alone. I glance around. The sound of the horde just below the patio wall makes my skin crawl. I realize, looking down at myself, how much gore and blood covers my body.

How long had I been like this? Like them, I wonder? I press my face against the slats of the wall, focusing on the moving creatures below. They look the same as ever. Rotted, broken.

I peel off my clothes, stiff and sticky, throwing them in the corner of the patio. The shower does me wonders, and when I emerge, I find a folded robe, undergarments, a sports bra, a large white tee shirt and a pair of sweatpants. Fine for now, but I'll have to find something more suitable before I go.

"There you go," she says, when I return to the living area. "You almost look cleaned up. Come and eat."

A bowl of the thick broth sits on the low table. The other bowl she holds in one hand. She gestures for me to sit.

"Feel better?" she asks.

"Much better. Thank you."

She doesn't speak to me as I eat. Ignoring the metal spoon, I pick up the bowl and inhale the rich broth, practically feeling the nutrients pouring into my body.

Once empty, she takes my bowl, returning to the burner and refilling it. After consuming this second bowl, this time a bit slower, I place it back on the table, wiping my mouth with the back of my hand.

She hands me a paper napkin. "Alright," she says. "I'd love to know how you pulled off a trick like that."

It takes me a little while to find my words again. Now that the adrenaline of the gun shot has died down, the inevitable fatigue sneaks up on me. The hot meal and clean clothes do their part. My eyes grow heavy.

"Oh, you poor thing!" she says, standing up and moving toward me. "You just lie down now. We can sort this all out later."

She leads me the few steps to the couch, placing one of the pillows under my head and covering me over with the yarn blanket. I manage to find my voice just before I drift off.

"How do you know?" I ask.

"Know what?"

"How do you know I wouldn't kill you?"

She chuckles, a throaty, honest sound. "Sweetie, I've seen a few things in my day. I had you spotted a few miles off, to tell the truth. Besides, if you was going to kill me, you'd a done it already. Now get some rest."

I barely realize I have already fallen asleep.

Fifteen

When I open my eyes, it takes me a minute to remember where I am. The sun streaming through the opening bathes the living space in a golden square of light.

My head hurts. My body feels stiff and sore. I hear the woman knocking about in the depths of the warehouse, items clattering here and there as she moves through the aisles. I struggle to sit up, but my muscles protest.

"Well, good mornin', Sunshine!" The woman emerges from the storage area, her arms laden with brown boxes. "How ya feelin'?"

I can only respond by placing my hand on my forehead, squinting my eyes against the brightness. She chuckles, making her way toward the stove. She pulls down a mug, pours steaming water from the kettle and scoops something from a small green tin into the mixture.

"Here, drink this. You'll feel better."

The hot liquid tastes bitter, but, I have to admit, it calms my stomach almost immediately. "What is this?" I manage.

"Tea. Earl Grey, actually. I sometimes think I have the only stash of it left in the whole world. Funny, that. But drink it on up. It's good for what ails you."

I pull myself up to sitting, curling my legs underneath me and wrapping the blanket over my lap. "And what ails me?" I ask. My throat feels sore, as if I'd been screaming. She does not answer right away but pours herself her own cup, before taking a seat on the chair across from me.

"Did you dream?" she asks. She sits forward, resting her elbows on her knees, folding her fingers together.

"I don't think so. I don't remember anything."

"That's good," she says. "That's a good thing. Means you're coming back to us."

I drink my tea, warmed enough now for me to take a larger swallow. The heat feels good, centering. "I… Have you seen this before?" I ask.

"Yup. I don't understand the hows or the whys, but I seen it. What's your name?"

"Ash."

"I'm Dottie."

"Can you help me, Dottie?"

"I reckon I can."

"What's happened to me?"

"Well," she rubs her hand across her cheek as she looks me over, "near as I can tell, you'd gone over. You'd turned somehow. But not all the way."

"How could that be?"

"Don't rightly know, Ash. You ain't been bit. That's for sure."

"No, I haven't."

"Yup. Only one thing to do if you'd been bit."

"What's that?" I ask absently.

"Put a bullet in you."

A sharp pain doubles me over. My arms clutch around my torso instinctively. "My stomach…"

"Yeah. You'll most likely have a sour stomach for a few days. Best to stay on easy foods for now until you get your strength back. I mean, your regular strength, that is."

"My regular strength?"

"Oh yes. You're stronger right now, most likely. Coming back is the hardest part."

I finish the rest of my tea, setting the cup down on the table. "How do you know all this?"

She shrugs. "A woman came through some time ago. Had a boy with her. He wasn't right. She helped bring him back. Like I said, I don't quite know the hows and the whys. But I'll keep you fed. Give you a place to sleep until you get your feet back under you."

"Thank you. Really, thank you."

"Don't mention it."

I pick up the pillow and tuck it behind me, enough that I have something on which to rest my head. "What happened... to the boy?"

"Oh, he got through it in the end. He was worse off than you, truth be told. I'd never seen anything like it. Saw them coming a mile away. I nearly took them down. My aim's got pretty good, you know."

"I believe you." I gently touch the binding around my arm.

"But she had him in some kind of hold. Hollered up at me not to shoot 'im. That she had it under control, all that kind of thing. If she hadn't been carrying on so, I would have taken both of them down.

"But that kid... Once we got him inside, we got him fed. He ate like he'd never seen a meal before. Just like you did. Then he slept for nearly fourteen hours. The woman said she sprung him from some kind of facility. I don't know. The idea that they're doing experiments like that makes me glad I don't go out much. You know anything about that? Experiments?"

"Experiments?" I pause, glancing up at her eyes. "No, I don't."

"Hm." She stood, brushing her hands across the front of her jeans. "Well, I reckon you'll need some supplies. Weapons and the like."

I realize with a sudden pang my backpack and crossbow are gone. I couldn't even retrace my steps to find them if I wanted to. I don't even know how far I've traveled or how many days I'd been out of it. Damn. That was a really good crossbow.

"I've got more guns in here than Fort Knox," she says, gesturing toward the shadows of the warehouse. "You're welcome to what you can use."

"What's Fort Knox?" I ask.

She chuckles, shaking her head. "Don't worry about it. Once you get your feet under you, you're welcome to have a look around. See what you can use."

"No guns," I say as I stretch out my arms.

"What's that?"

"I don't use guns."

"Huh. You don't use guns? Why not?"

"They make too much noise. Ends up drawing more of them. It's not worth it, really."

"Well yeah. There's that, I suppose. Suit yourself. There's plenty of everything back there. I'm going to make my rounds. There's bread and cheese in the pantry there. Help yourself to anything you might find. I'll be back in about an hour."

She disappears into the shadows, the sound of her footsteps on the metal staircase echoes back to me. I am alone, for the first time in… I don't know how long.

I swing my legs around, placing my feet on the floor. Testing my balance, I stand, steadying my hand against the arm of the couch. So far so good.

Dottie has managed to create the illusion of coziness within the vast space. She had positioned the chairs and couch in a small square with the stove and cabinets against the nearest wall. I make my way toward the pantry area, a collection of shelves laden with various canned foods, bags of oats, and some boxes of something called Malt o' Meal.

I find a peel-top can of fish drenched in some kind of

sauce. I eat it with my fingers. It's not much, but the food calms my stomach, and it tastes good. After wiping down my face and hands, I pick up one of the many flashlights set in a row on the shelf.

I wander down the aisle, swinging the light up and down the shelves. The silence envelopes me the deeper I get into the warehouse, with the dim light as my only companion. A feeling of vertigo taunts my balance. Shelves soaring overhead, the aisles nothing more than darkened hallways plunging into the distance.

Each shelf contains huge cardboard boxes, each nearly the size of a small car, wrapped in a clear plastic cellophane. Some of these had been sliced open, the contents picked through, divided up. I could see where she gathered the supplies she needed from the available fare. Food, clothing, furniture, all stored neatly here in this vast concrete storehouse.

Aisle after aisle I roam. The place feels like a mausoleum, a remnant of a forgotten world. Now and then, I examine the items displayed within the boxes. Some of it makes sense: salt and pepper shakers, paper towels, and so on. Other things, not so much. Curling irons, scented pine cones, something called bumpo seats… By the time I make my way back to the living area, Dottie had returned, polishing her weapons at the table.

"Help yourself to anything you find useful," she said. "There's plenty there. I imagine this place will still be full of useless stuff long after all of us are gone."

"How did you find this place?" I take a seat on the couch, the blanket still draped over the corner.

She chuckles, placing her gun to the side, crossing her hands in front of her. "It's a funny story, that," she says. "You sure you want to hear it?"

I pull the blanket over my legs. "I've got nowhere to be."

"The truth is, I never left," she says.

"What?"

"Yeah. I was the Operations Manager here for sixteen years before the shit hit the fan. I don't know, I hardly ever went home. Didn't have a family or anything, so I threw everything I had into my job. I thought at the time that's what I was supposed to do."

"You didn't have a boyfriend?"

She shakes her head with a small chuckle. "Never was much of the boyfriend type."

"Or… a girlfriend?" I venture.

Her smile widens for a moment, gazing wistfully out the open entrance. "Maybe more my type, but I was too old by the time that became socially acceptable."

All of a sudden, a wave of fatigue washes over. She must see it because she stands up and gathers her weapons. "You get some rest now," she says. "It's going to be another day or two before you feel quite yourself."

"Yeah," I reply. "I'd better."

She carries away her stash, leaving me alone in the living area. I pull the blanket around my shoulders, lying back on the arm of the couch, positioned so I can see to the outside through the doorway. Sleep falls on me quickly and there is only darkness.

A new pile of clothing and supplies greets me when I wake. It feels like morning. Did I sleep through the night, I wonder? Dottie is nowhere to be seen in the immediate area. A small handwritten note sits on top of the folded clothes.

> *Ash,*
> *Gone out. I left some*
> *coffee in the machine. All*
> *you have to do is push the*

button and it will brew in a
minute. Also, help yourself
to whatever food you find.
-D

I do so, wrapping the blanket around my shoulders to stave off the morning chill. After setting the coffee to brew, I poke around in the pantry. This time I manage to find a sleeve of crackers to go along with another tin of fish. And then another.

Next, I locate a bowl of apples tucked behind the boxes. I eat three of them. Followed by a box of something called "star crunch."

Dottie finds me about an hour later. Blood covers her arms up to her elbows and she carries a brace of hares in each hand. I sit on the floor, peering up at her, my back leaning against the doors of the cabinets eating the last morsel out of a bag of spiced jerky.

"Well, looks like you got your appetite back," she says dryly, placing the rabbits down on the countertop.

I glance around myself, noticing for the first time the mess of package wrappers and empty boxes surrounding me. "Sorry..." I mutter.

"Don't be. It's a good sign actually. Means you've turned the corner."

"Turned the corner?" I take her extended hand and pull up, onto my feet.

"You're on the path to recovery, I'd say." She pulls a Bowie knife from her belt. "Now help me skin these rabbits and we'll have another good meal this afternoon."

A few hours pass and we have a pot of stew boiling cheerfully on the stove. The lights directly above us flicker in three slow strobes.

"Dammit!" she exclaims, reaching out and turning down the stove. "Stay here and watch the soup. We got company."

"The hell I will," I say, tossing aside the blanket and following behind her. We scurry up the staircase, through the door, and onto the roof.

"See? There." She points off into the wooded distance. "They've triggered the periphery."

"Is it zombies? How many?"

"Not zombies. Worse."

"What could be worse than zombies?" I ask.

She chambers the gun. "Men."

The first time I had seen her, she had stood straight up with both feet planted firmly beneath her, picking off the zombies one by one, making no effort to hide her presence. This time, she quickly dropped, hiding behind the short wall surrounding the roof. I follow her lead, keeping my head low but still able to see just over the edge.

"What are you doing to do?" I whisper.

"That depends on what *they* do? Just sit tight and don't make any noise."

Five men emerge from the forest's edge. They appear a rough sort, leathery skin and steely eyes, hardened by living in the elements. They pace the edge of the building, keeping their distance and eyeing the multiple entrances. Dottie does not fire, but she keeps her eye on the scope. Every few seconds, she lifts her eyes, looking them over.

The idea suddenly frightened me that she might shoot them. Her shotgun had a makeshift silencer on the barrel, but still I didn't trust the discharge of the weapon not to draw the zombies.

But she never shoots. She just waits, watching as the men below circle around the building, three going one way and two headed toward the other.

"What do we do?" I whisper.

"Shh!" She pulls back down to the base of the wall, turning towards me. "They're looking to see if the building is occupied."

"Well? Is it?"

She slowly grins, a mischievous twinkle forming in her eyes. "They're about to find out."

Sixteen

The men disappear from view, stepping closer to building. I had not gotten a good look at the front of the building when I had arrived. I had entered from the truck entrance on the side, so I have no idea what or where they are approaching.

Dottie waits, focused and listening. I stay still, waiting, watching for her next action. The men have vanished beneath the wall. Seconds go by. I don't know what we are waiting for.

Someone screams.

Dottie chuckles, her shoulders trembling.

"What did you do?" I ask with some skepticism.

"Shh. Wait for it."

The men, all five of them, run out of the building not looking back. They keep running for as long as we can see them, vanishing into the overgrown forests.

Dottie's amusement creeps out from the corners of her eyes, her mirth unbridled.

"Dottie," I press. "*What* did you do?"

She hops to her feet, extending a hand to help me up.

"Come on. I'll show you."

This time, we take the stairs down to a lower level. Where the other floor is comprised of organized rows, this one appeared as a jumble of machinery. A metal conveyor snakes through the various contraptions, most of which have lain dormant for some time based on the layer of dust covering them.

Dottie leads me through this space along the side of the room. Wide yellow arrows mark the places to safely walk, surrounded by red stripes with the word "danger" emblazoned at the edges.

"This place always made such a racket when we were still

in production," Dottie says. "But we kept the record for least number of incidents in the tri-county area."

"I don't know what that means," I reply.

"Eh, don't worry about it," she chuckles. "It's not worth explaining."

We turn a corner, heading down a long hallway and into a room furnished with a desk and small, padded chairs lining the facing wall. Glass double doors and a panel of windows flood the room with sunlight.

"This here's the only entrance to this part of the building," she says.

"What about the other way?" I ask. "The way you brought me in?"

"That has to be run from the inside. If it's closed up, it looks just like the rest of the cargo bay doors. No one in or out unless someone is there to work the lift, and that someone is me."

"I see." I follow her around the edge of the tiny office. She reaches underneath the desk, triggering something with a faint click.

"I have to reset it every time," she says. "That's the only downside. It takes about half the day, but it's worth it for the security. Come on."

We make our way back into the machine room. The dim light illuminated the room from the base of the walls, casting otherworldly shadows across the contraptions.

Dottie lifts something bulky from the end of the conveyor belt, wrapping her arms around it and heaving it up onto the surface. Now I see it is a mannequin body, a legless thing with arms jutting at an awkward angle, its bald head and painted eyes staring at nothing.

"Do you need a hand with anything?" I ask.

"Nah. I've done this enough times, I've got the routine

down to a science."

"What exactly is all this?"

She replaces the mannequin at the far end, facing the entrance. "Now where did I put it last time?" Rummaging in the space underneath, she pulls out a roll of red plastic tape. "Ah, here we go."

"What's that for?" I ask.

"I tie it along here. When the belt goes, it kicks up a wind. The red blows around and makes it look like a fire."

"A fire…" I try to picture what she describes.

"A real fire is too risky of course, but with the lights and the mannequins, it's usually enough to scare people off." She proceeds into tying strips of the red plastic to the corners and edges of the conveyor belt and along the edges of the rollers. I picture it from the perspective of the men, most likely still running for their lives in the middle of the wilds.

"What made me think of it," she continues, "there was an accident here, before my time of course. But this young man, full of vinegar, thought he could get away with pulling a prank. Sorry for him it was the last thing he ever did."

"What happened?"

"Dumb little shit thought he could come down the belt on his knees like this and scare his co-workers. Got his pants caught in the gears, here." She gestures to the machinery underneath. "Then, this part here malfunctioned and the sparks caught fire. He never had a chance."

"Oh my god."

"Yeah. He was gone before they could even pull the emergency stop. They barely scraped enough of him together to have something to bury."

I shiver at the description, falling silent as she continues, speaking in a matter-of-fact tone as she works her way around the room.

"That's one reason they hired me up. I was always that one who did things by the book. Said I could clean this place up, get the safety back up to standard. And I did too. Highest safety rating in the tri-county area."

"Yeah," I reply quietly.

She worked steadily, tying red tape along the corners all around the room, placing mannequins at the edges to create the macabre illusion of flaming torsos. I stay, but keep my distance. Her work here feels like something which should not be interrupted, something ceremonial, in a way.

"You know," she says, turning back toward me after her last task. "I was in this very building when the shit hit the fan."

"Were you?"

"Yeah." Her eyes grow distant. "Down that very hallway. I didn't even know at first what had happened. Barely watched any teevee most days. Then people started calling in sick. Three on the first day. I just thought they'd gone out drinkin'. But then the next day ten more didn't show. By the fourth day I had no one to run the place.

"I called in to corporate to get approval for the temp replacements, and no one answered. It just kept going to a busy signal. No one answered. I went home that day. Came back the next morning. Same story. No one showed. Took me a whole week to realize something had happened.

"And, here, I'd missed the whole thing. Wadn't till a whole horde of nasties came up over the horizon that I realized the shit had indeed hit the fan."

I see the memory of it on her face. "What did you do?" I ask.

She chuckled, shaking her head. "I bunked up. Once I realized they couldn't get past the front door, I took some time to barricade the entrances. With the warehouse upstairs, I've got more than enough supplies." She reaches out, tapping the flat of her palm against the wall. "A real bonafide fortress right under my feet."

"You've been here ever since?"

"Yep. Couldn't have built a better place to ride out the apocalypse."

"What's next?"

"I dunno. Been doing fine so far. No need to change what ain't broken."

"No... I meant... The room. What's next to finish, setting up the room."

"Oh, right!" she exclaims, glancing around. "It's done. Yeah. They walk in the front door. Hit the trip wire and boom, flaming torsos coming from all directions."

I raise an eyebrow. "Effective."

"More than you know. Come on. Soup should be done by now."

An hour later, we strip the meat from the bones of the boiled rabbits after they cooled on the counter. After shredding the meat back into the broth, she popped open a can of carrots and peas, letting them simmer. She pours a bowl for each of us, handing one over to me before settling into her chair across from me.

"Why me?" I ask.

"Why you, what?" she replies around a bit of food.

"Why'd you bring me in and not them?"

"Ah." She takes another bite. "I don't know. You just kind of get a sense after a while. Besides, I don't let in the menfolk. First couple of years I did my best to help anyone who crossed my path. But after a while I started to notice a pattern."

"Yeah? What kind of pattern?"

"I figured out pretty quickly, there were two types of travelers. Some are just looking for a way station, a place to rest up, refill their water bottles. Maybe take a day or two off their feet, that kind of thing."

"And the other?"

"The other," she chuckles. "The other kind… They want to take what you have. For no other reason than because you have it and they don't."

"And that's what inspired the flaming torsos?" I ask.

"No. No, I didn't come up with that until about three years ago. First I tried to fight them off. Got plenty of weapons in this place. Did alright at first, but the noise drew more trouble than I could handle."

"Zombies."

"Yep. Zombies."

"I lost my weapons I guess," I say. "I'm assuming I didn't have any on me when you found me."

"No, hun. I'm afraid not."

"Figures. I had a crossbow. Worked like a charm."

She stands up and takes my empty bowl, placing them both on the counter. "You know what?" she says. "Come with me. I got something to show you."

"Alright."

We walk down the center aisle toward the back of the warehouse. It feels like a mile at least, though I know it's far less. The forced perspective, the straight lines of the shelving stretching ahead, makes the space feel surreal.

"Here we are," she says once we arrive at the back wall, dimly lit by the remnants of sunlight struggling to break through the shadows. "For a while I didn't know what to do with myself, so I started cataloging the inventory. Got most things separated out. Figuring out what I can use and so forth. This here's where I keep the weapons. Guns, knives, crossbows. Take your pick."

It is glorious, the feast of weaponry displayed before me. Gleaming metal, polished wood reflecting the sparse illumination.

Alongside the massive collection of handguns, hunting rifles, and semi-automatics, the wall contains blades, arrows, and more melee weapons than I have seen in one place.

"Wow," I murmur. "Where did all this come from?"

"Just part of the inventory," she replies. "This warehouse moved more supplies during my lifetime than I can count. We happen to supply a major chain of sporting goods on the east coast. I couldn't have stocked this place better if I'd planned for it."

"I'd say so."

She glances me over and an amused smile plays across her face. "You help yourself to whatever you need. I'm going to go ahead and do my rounds."

I still have my knife, ignored and strapped to my ankle during my time with the undead, but I add another for good measure. The selection of crossbows is not quite as large as that of the hunting rifles, but there is still much to choose from. I take stock of each one, lifting it to my eye and feeling the weight of it in my hands until I find the right one.

Perfect fit against my shoulder with a strap around my chest, resting snug on my back. I smile briefly, looking forward to breaking this one in.

The lights flicker, just like they had done before. Dottie calls out to me from across the warehouse. "We got company!"

"Again?" I reply.

"To the roof, double time!"

We are met with a view of three, two men and one woman, running at full tilt toward the front of the warehouse.

145

Dottie peers through the scope, switching immediately to the binoculars for a closer look.

"Holy shit," she mutters as she squints through the viewfinder. "I know them." She stands up, waving her arms overhead. The woman edges ahead by a few feet, cheeks red with exertion.

"Bogies coming in behind us, Dot!" she calls. "We need a door!"

"Down front! I've got you covered!" Dottie calls back, swinging her weapon into place, aiming for the forest line.

Within seconds the zombies emerge, half a dozen moving at a surprising speed, keeping pace with their quarry in herky-jerky steps. Dottie focuses, closing her other eye and taking aim.

"Wait!" I say, placing my hand on her shoulder. The unmistakable faded yellow dress differentiates Penny from the others, shuffling at a steady clip at the back of the cluster, her gait just as determined as the rest of them.

"You wanna tell me what I'm waitin' for?" Dottie snaps.

"Just..." I scramble to find the right words. "Get your friends inside. I'll handle the rest of them."

Dottie hesitates, eyeing me with suspicion. She doesn't move until I pull around my newly acquired crossbow.

"Go," I say. "I got this."

She disappears down the stairs. I aim, peering through the scope but keeping my finger off the trigger. In this manner, I focus my mind. Reaching desperately for a connection with them. Penny connects first, her frantic wisps of mental abstraction surging into my consciousness.

"There you are," I whisper, pushing gently back against her trajectory. She slows her steps, shuffling to a stop. "Okay, now the rest of you." I reach, a dull ache blooming at the base of my skull. "Come on..."

The leading zombie lurches forward, just inches behind the last man running from them. Its jangly arms flailing from his torso, gnashing exaggerated teeth.

I hear the door open below me, Dottie calling for the people to get inside. I have to slow down the zombies or they won't make it.

"Shoot them!" Dottie yells. "Shoot them now!"

I take aim, still reaching for purchase for the other zombies, desperate to connect. Like tumblers falling into place, the connection opens up.

The zombies stumble, slowing to a standstill just as the newcomers disappear inside, the door slamming shut. I collapse against the wall, catching my breath as I pull the crossbow to my chest.

I had held the zombies back just long enough for Dottie to get her people inside.

Seventeen

Making my way down the stairs to the warehouse, I hear them before I see them, the newly arrived guests. Voices arguing, tumbling over each other for purchase.

"What did she do?"

"Why didn't she shoot them?"

"How did she do that?"

"What happened out there?"

"Enough!" This one is Dottie, interrupting the melee. "The important thing is, you got inside. Now, I imagine y'all are wanting something to eat?"

"Dot," the woman says, speaking quieter now. "She stopped them, but she didn't shoot them. How did she do it?"

Dottie does not reply. I wait until they move into the living area before I emerge from the staircase. They all appear road weary, but still flushed from the adrenaline of the chase.

The woman sits across from Dottie, long dusty blonde hair pulled into a low ponytail. One of the men, the fairer of the two, sits on the corner chair, perched at the edge, eyes darting between the two women.

The other man paces behind them, stretching out his arms and occasionally shaking one leg and then the other. Working out the adrenaline. I've done a similar routine myself on occasion.

When I emerge from the shadows of the staircase, they fall silent at the sight of me, each looking at me with wary, suspicious eyes. Dottie had dished each of them out a bowl of food, all of which sit untouched on the table.

"Come on," she gestures me over. "It's alright. Ash, this here's Sadie, Rodge, and Ian. I've known these three for near as long as the world's been done. Come on and have a seat. You may want to hear what they have to say." I do so, feeling like a specimen under a microscope more so than I had in a long time.

"Things are bad out there," Sadie says. "I'm going to tell you right now, I've seen a lot of things. But I ain't never seen anything like what you just did out there. But if Dottie says you're okay, then I guess you're okay."

"I appreciate it," I reply, meeting her gaze. "How bad is it out there?"

The woman picks up the bowl in front of her, taking a few large bites before speaking again. "We've been as far as the Mississippi before we turned back. Everything west of the river is gone, overtaken by those things as far as the eye can see. If there's any survivors over there, they're on their own."

Dottie nods, her forehead drawn together. The pacing man takes a seat, and everyone finally turns their attention to their food.

Sadie continues. "We see pockets of survivors out and about this side of the mountains. They all say the same thing. The zombies are getting faster, pooling together in larger hordes than before. It's hard to say what's caused the differences. They're evolving somehow. It's rather unsettling."

"I know what's caused it," I say. "Or rather, who."

Everyone's eyes snap in my direction.

"The woman in the tower?" Sadie asks.

"Yes," I reply. "How do you know?"

This time Rodge speaks up. "As we've gotten closer to this area we've heard tell of her behavior. People gone missing, turning up after, but… turned. You know."

"Turned?" Dottie asks.

"Yeah," Sadie nods. "Turned into one of them, but different even than what we've seen. Like those out there, faster, meaner. It's been gotten harder to get away from them. Harder to keep away from them."

"Like the ones outside," Dottie says, turning her gaze toward me with a knowing expression.

"Yeah," I say, nodding. "Like the ones outside."

The other man, Ian, broke his silence, speaking in a tense high-pitched voice, leveling his gaze in my direction. "Anybody want to explain to me what happened out there? Why did they stop? What aren't you telling us?"

I glance at Dottie. She nods for me to continue. "I stopped them," I reply. "With my mind."

"You did what?" Sadie chimed.

"See, I know her. She raised me, for lack of a better term. When the virus got loose, some of the people at the laboratory helped me escape. They did this at the cost of their lives. I'll never be able to pay that back."

Sadie's eyes widen. "I've heard of you," she says. "The Untouchable Girl. Never thought I'd see you do your thing live and in person."

"So," Ian leans forward, elbows resting on his knees. "Just exactly how *do* you do your thing?"

I reach up, placing my fingertips at the base of my skull feeling along the edge of the coin-shaped implant. "She did it," I reply. "I found her again, this last year. I thought if I confronted her... I don't know what I thought. But while I was there, she put something in my head that makes me... like them. Makes me connect to them on some kind of level. I don't even understand it myself really."

"Can I see?" Sadie asks.

I pull my hair aside, revealing the back of my head. She stands and approaches. With tentative fingers she feels where I guide her along the edge of my hairline. The sensation of her touching my neck gives me shivers. I shift my shoulders to hide the fact.

"About the size of a quarter I'd say," she says, taking her seat again. "It's right at the surface, but there's a lot of nerves right there."

"How does it work?" Ian asks.

"I don't know," I reply. "But I think it somehow connects me to them. Mentally. It makes me control them, somehow." I wonder if they can tell I am leaving out a lot of details.

"Does it always work?" Rodge asks.

"No, not always. If I'm weak, like if food is scarce or I haven't slept enough, it doesn't work as well."

Sadie speaks again. "So, have you been out there since you were a child? How could that be?"

I shrug. "I just try to get through one day at a time, you know. Keeping to myself most of the time, learning as I go. Foraging, scavenging. I've had help along the way. People like Dottie. People out there help each other more often than not."
Sadie nods, her eyes soften as she glances towards Dottie. "Yeah. That much is true."

"How do you know each other?" I ask.

"I've known Dottie from early on," Sadie says. "About a year in, I'd say."

"That sounds right," Dottie answers. "It's hard to keep track of the time anymore. Running from that horde. That was the biggest crowd of them I'd seen up to then. It's a good thing I saw you when I did."

"Some things never change." Sadie finished her bowl and set it down on the table.

Ian suppresses a yawn, placing the heels of his hands against his eyes.

Dottie stands up, brushing her hands across her legs. "You three are probably exhausted. Let me get you set up with a place to sleep."

"You still got that shower contraption?" Rodge asks. "I could do with that."

"You know I do," Dottie says with a smile. "Come on. I'll find you some towels."

Dottie gathers up the empty bowls and places them in the sink. She and the others wander toward the interior of the aisles gathering items for their stay. I sneak away, making my way back to the roof.

There they stand, just at the edge of the forest, as still and straight as the tin soldiers in a childhood story I'd once read, no more than five all together.

Her yellow dress burns bright in the light of the setting sun, stark against the shadowy backdrop of the forest. Her gray, decaying skin appeared almost luminescent in the fading light, sunken cheeks and milky eyes.

I feel her mental connection almost immediately. Penny reaching out to me, clicking into place. Her proximity remains a wordless void, ever present in my mind, reaching, searching, desperate for something only I can seemingly offer.

A few minutes later, I sense Dottie approaching behind me. She watches me from a short distance away, hovering at the roof's door. I already know, under normal circumstances, her eyes would be trained on them, but these are not normal circumstances.

"Did your friends get situated?" I ask.

"Yes. I'll set them up with another sleeping area towards the back. I've got a number of futons we can pull out for them. What do... they want?" she asks, her voice betraying the uncertainty of the scenario laid out before us.

"It's hard to say, really," I reply.

"Do they know you're here?"

"I'm sure they do. I don't know if they meant to find me,

but it seems they have."

"They're waiting for you?"

I turn, glancing at her briefly before casting my eyes to the ground between us. "Oh, yes. They are. Of that there is no doubt."

"What will you do?"

I take a breath to answer her, but lightning strikes, a pain surges through my head. White hot, blinding. Clutching at my temples I fall to my knees, eyes squeezed shut. Dottie nearly catches me, clutching my forearms to steady me.

"Oh dear, what is this? Are you all right?"

"Yes," I say. "Just one of my headaches. I get them sometimes. It will fade in a minute."

"Let's head back. We've still got some hot bone broth. That would do you some good, I'm sure."

"No, no. I'm fine, really." I take a moment, allowing her to steady me back to my feet. "Please. I'm sure your guests are wondering where you've gone. I'll be fine, really. I promise."

"You're sure?"

"Yes. If I could have a minute…"

She takes a step back, glancing toward Penny and the others. "Of course." Dottie disappears down the stairs without another word. Her back recedes into the shadows. I already know what I need to do, but the less they know, the better.

After night falls, I gather my things. The men are sleeping, but I hear Dottie and Sadie still up, having a quiet conversation on the landing.

I slip out behind them, down the stairs, walking carefully to avoid any trip wires along the way. I don't want my last gift to Dottie to be having to reset her contraptions again.

The air holds a familiar chill, brisk against my cheeks and hands. My eyes train on Penny and her entourage, centurions at the watch. Once more I check over my weapons, knives, bow, backpack slung over one shoulder, heavy with supplies gathered over the last few days.

I have a hike in front of me. That much I do know. Though I don't know where I am or which direction I need to start.

Crossing the field towards the forest's edge, a slight mist dampens my skin, not quite enough to be rain, but more than a heavy dew.   My hair sticks to my face and neck.

I am grateful for the clean clothes and extra socks tucked in my bag. Dottie's warehouse had been just the respite I needed, but the time had come to move on.

Once I reach Penny and the others, I can see the increase in decay taking over. Her mouth appears drawn back against protruding teeth. Sunken eyes and paper-thin cheeks, not much left but skin and bones.

Her body does not fare much better. Muscles sheared off, revealing edges of bones tinged with dark blood.

Yet, she looks at me, milky, vacant eyes. My connection with her mind feels like a beacon in my head, a macabre lighthouse leading me forward.

"Okay Penny," I say. "Where we headed?"

She turns, apparently satisfied that I will follow, and takes the few steps into the shadows of the forest. The others follow along with her, shuffling steps, torn shoes catching against leaves and roots.

I follow, picking up my knees and ducking under the branches, bare bony fingers reaching for me. The rain picks up, falling on the seven of us in cold steady streams.

Eighteen

We follow the ravine, nothing more than a motley crew of myself and a handful of zombies. When we arrive at the water's edge. I take a moment to refill my canteen and check my weapons.

The zombies mill around, largely ignoring me. I can't estimate how far we have come since leaving the warehouse. My headache has all but vanished. Being here, with these creatures, feels strangely comforting. A short time later, we crest the horizon and the farm comes into view.

"How are we going to do this?" I mutter. They don't respond, just shuffling in place with those blank eyes and rotting faces. "Yeah, okay. We'll just see how this goes."

The closer we get, the more details of the farm come into view. Tents and sleeping mats map out the space surrounding the house, most of them facing toward the fire pit.

A young boy at the edge of the circle spots me, one of the kids from Fairlight's group. He stands, motioning to me, to the others.

I can't imagine what I must look like, broken and covered in dust, surrounded by the undead. He calls out, rushing toward the house.

I see Ezekiel stepping from the shadows of the house and out onto the porch, shadowing his eyes against the sun. I walk toward the outer gate, arriving across from him at the opposite gate. He watches me from the expanse between us, studying my movements.

"Ash?" he calls.

"I'm okay," I reply, hoping my voice sounds steady. I offer a wave. He motions for the others to stay back, curiosity drawing them a few steps closer. He eyes me, skeptical.

"I'm okay," I call again. "Can I come in?"

Finally, he lifts his keys, opening the padlock and pulling the inner gate far enough for him to step through. I've never felt more like a pariah.

Ezekiel crosses the distance between us until we stand face to face, only the metal links of the fence between us.

"What happened?" he asks.

"Yeah, I'm not exactly sure."

"Did you get bit?"

"Do I look that bad? "No, I'm not bit."

He gestures toward the small horde behind me. "What's this about?"

I glance at them, hunched and lurching. "They won't hurt anyone as long as I'm around."

His eyes cut to the side. "How do you figure?"

"Look, can you let me in? I promise I can explain everything. And I'd love to get cleaned up. They'll stay out here, obviously."

"Fine," he says, patting his holster. "But I promise, if anything goes south I'm taking them out."

"They're not the enemy, Ezekiel."

"No?"

"No."

He pulls the outer gate open. I don't like the sound of him threatening the zombies. They are just victims like the rest of us. But I need him on my side. I hold my tongue. Once the gates are locked behind us, we head toward the fire.

"How's Thorn?" I ask, trying to keep my eyes forward.

"He's good. He's better. Once we got settled here, Fairlight was able to gather more ingredients to fortify his system. He's still healing, but he's up and about. He'll be around, I'm sure. Come on." He takes off toward the group of people gathered around the fire.

I stop, painfully aware of my appearance. "I don't think-- Look, is Fairlight here? I should speak to her."

He pauses and turns, seeing my hesitation. "Yeah, she's here. I'll go get her."

I hang back, waiting next to the maple tree halfway between the fence and the house. Ezekiel runs over to the porch, calling inside.

Fairlight emerges, followed by Thorn. He leaves the two of them speaking to each other and makes his way over to me.

Thorn. Healthy. Whole. Healed.

I want nothing more than to run to him, but I remember the reflection of myself in the pond, pale eyes, sallow flesh, and the blood. I gaze down at my hands. He can't see me like this.

I do my best to stay in the shadows underneath the tree, but I can't hide from him forever. He trots over to me, a look of palpable relief on his face.

"Are you okay?" he asks as he nears.

I lower my face, but he steps forward, reaches for my chin to lift my face to his.

"Let me see you, Ash. What's happened?"

"Don't," I say, pulling my face away. "It's not what you think."

"Why not? Ash, what's happened? Talk to me."

"It's-- It's hard to explain. I'm not bit, if that's what you think."

He takes a step back. "I don't think anything, Ash."

I muster up the strength to glance up, meeting his eyes for a second before I retreat to the safety of staring at the ground. I guess I owe him some kind of explanation, at least.

"I, um... I'm connected to them somehow. More than

159

what I thought. I can't explain it except that I kind of… hear them. I don't know."

He takes my chin, lifting my face and peering into my eyes, searching. I cannot bring myself to look at him directly. I try to move my face away, but he holds me on place, examining me.

Despite my expectation, I see no revulsion in his expression. Perhaps curiosity but nothing more. Finally, he lets go, moving his hand from his rough hold on my chin to a softer clasp at the base of my hair. All the while keeping my gaze caught with his own.

"This isn't over, is it?" he asks.

I shake my head once.

"Ash. I'll be here, if… *When* you come back. I promise. But whatever this is… You need to figure it out."

I cannot speak. I reach up, placing my hand over his and gently move it away.

"You could stay, you know," he continues. "Just let it go and come back with us."

"Thorn, I have to go back. You know that."

Our conversation dies out as Fairlight approaches, Ezekiel a few steps behind her. She looks me over, her forehead twisted in confusion.

"I'm not a threat," I say, extending out my palms.

"Honestly, it's worse than it looks."

"What is it?" she asks. "What's happened to you?"

"She's done this somehow. The doctor. But I'm still… I'm still me, Fairlight."

She turns to the other two. "Could you leave us for a moment," she says. This is not a question but a command, despite her tone. They leave, Ezekiel giving me a wary glance before turning his attention away.

Once alone, she wordlessly looks me over, examining the

details of my face and arms, cradling my hands in hers. The sickly pallor of my complexion contrasts stark against her healthy pink skin. I can sense the repugnance in her touch. I don't blame her. I would be too.

"I'm going back, you know," I say. "I can control them somehow. More than I could before, somehow. I'm not sure why."

"Go on," she says.

"She's created a beacon, some kind of frequency she emits from the central tower. That's how she controls them. Hundreds of them at once. It's some sort of subsonic emission. I don't quite understand it."

"Why did you come back here?" Fairlight asks, her voice clipped and cold. "Why not stay and finish the job?"

"Because I need your help."

Fairlight lowered her hands, watching me carefully.

"I know why I've been having these headaches."

"What is it, Ash?"

Tentatively, I reach for her hand. She lets me place her fingertips just at the base of my skull. "I didn't feel it at first because I have a lumpy skull right there, but once you know it's there..." Her gaze goes soft as she runs the pads of her fingers over the disc.

"Ash. How did...?"

"She must have put it in there when she had me in the compound. They ran so many tests on me, I couldn't keep track of them all. I can't help wonder what else she did to me."

"I see." She lowers her hand.

"Can you take it out?" I ask.

She thinks for a moment, her pale brow pinched together. "It would be very painful. We don't have any way to make you comfortable."

"I can handle pain," I whisper.

"Ash, it would be quite dangerous. If something went wrong…"

"Fairlight, can you do it?" I meet her eyes, keeping my gaze steady. After another moment, she speaks.

"Yes. I can do it."

I'm laid out on the cot in the panic room. Ezekiel fetches Abraham's old medical kit, a cracked leather black bag with a brass handle.

I sense Thorn hovering upstairs, outside the door. He has been tasked with making sure the house remains vacant during the procedure. Everyone else has gone outside under strict instructions from Fairlight until further notice.

"Have you done this before?" I say, my head turned to the side as I lie on my stomach.

"Not exactly," Fairlight replies.

She places the items out onto a small table next to her, a bottle of alcohol, gauze, bandages, a shaving razor, a pair of scissors, a wooden spoon, and, finally, Ezekiel's knife. He had sharpened it on his whetstone before holding the blade into the fire to sterilize it.

"You'll have to be still," she continues.

"Ezekiel will help," I say. "Won't you?" He nods, taking his place at the top of the cot.

"I'm going to shave this area here on the back of your head," Fairlight says. "Just so you know what I'm doing. I'll tell you as we go, okay?"

"Yeah, okay." I press my lips together, pressing my forehead into the cot.

She lifts my hair, snipping it away as close to the skin as she can. I hear the tufts landing on the floor as she tosses them out of the way.

The cold blade of the razor meets my skin, scraping bare the back of my head. She smooths a warm washcloth over my skin, followed by a swab of alcohol over the whole area.

"Okay Ash," she says. "Are you ready?"

Ezekiel takes the wooden spoon from the table. I open my mouth and allow him to place the handle between my teeth.

I meet his eyes as he does so, finding in that moment a spark of trust between us. He will hold me steady, no matter what.

He crouches down, placing his hands on either side of my head. I reach forward and clasp my hands around his forearms.

"I got you, Ash," he whispers.

"Okay," I say. "I'm ready."

The knife blade touches my skin. The pain is like nothing I have ever felt. Teeth clench around the wooden bit, my jaw seizing, and eyes squeezed shut.

I hear a voice, Ezekiel saying something, speaking directly into my ear.

He sounds miles away.

Something pulls against my scalp, pressure, pain, screaming, blinding pain. I feel myself falling, my whole body untethered. I am connected to nothing, and nothing holds me.

I'm falling.

Everything goes dark.

And I feel nothing.

When I wake, I am alone.

No, not alone. Someone's hand touches my forehead. Ezekiel? Fairlight? Somehow, I don't think either one of them capable of the gentleness apparent in this touch.

"Are you coming back to us?"

Great. It's Thorn.

My eyes flutter open. My head aches. I'm lying on my side.

"Take it easy," he says. "You've been through it, Ash."

"Is it gone?" I say, my voice not much more than a whispered rasp.

"It's gone."

"Oh, thank god," I mutter, reaching my hand back to feel the bandage.

"Does it hurt much?"

"It hurts like a bitch," I reply. "But I wouldn't want it any different. As long as it's out."

"Yeah." He glances back toward the stairs leading up to the open door. "Well, I should let you get some rest."

"Thorn, wait." I reach for him, my hand clasping his, almost of its own volition. He turns to look at me with a question in his eyes. "Will you stay? Just for a little while?"

He stays, leaning against the side of the cot, our fingers intertwined. His presence comforts me, enough at least that I can drift into a light sleep.

Even then, I sense him sitting there, his steady breathing, his warmth. I don't know how long he stays with me. I feel as if I'm in and out for hours, but each time my eyes open, he is there, his crooked smile and nervous eyes gazing softly at me.

"What must I look like?" I mutter.

"You look beautiful," he replies.

Once more I drift off into a dreamless sleep, his hand still curled comfortably into mine.

Nineteen

The pain subsides after a few days. Perhaps it is the steady diet of bone broth brought to me by Fairlight. I had moved up to the room where I used to stay.

What had once felt cozy and homey now just seemed cold and impersonal. The bed feels far more comfortable, however.

"It's healing rather quickly," Fairlight says, changing my bandage. "You'll have a nice scar, but it looks like you've avoided any infection."

"That's good," I say.

"How is the pain?"

"It's better. Not as bad as it has been."

"Just a quick swab," she says, dabbing area with a cotton gauze. I pull in my breath against the sting of alcohol. It only lasts for a moment, and she quickly secures a clean bandage into place.

"What did you do with it? The implant."

"Ezekiel's been studying the thing. He's got it in there with all of his equipment. Studying bandwidths and such. I don't quite understand it, but he's like a kid with a new toy."

"Good riddance. At least it's out of my head. What is he looking for, exactly?"

"Hard to say. He's looking for the frequency, is what he said."

With the new bandage in place, I turn over, careful to avoid pressure on the back of my head, curling my arms under my cheek. Fairlight takes a seat in the chair close to the edge of the bed.

"There was a bit of trouble yesterday," she says.

"Oh yeah? What kind of trouble?"

"Someone recognized one of your monsters. The one in

165

the yellow dress."

My face goes cold. "Penny."

"Her name is Saffron," Fairlight continues. "She was one of the first ones taken. Before we really understood what was going on. Her parents left us soon after. Said they joined us for the safety of it, and if we couldn't promise that they had no reason to stay. Whole thing was a bit messy."

"What happened? Yesterday, I mean. They didn't--"

"Your monsters are fine, if that's what you're worried about." Her voice takes on an icy tone. "A couple of the girls saw her. It upset them a bit. She was friends with them, you see."

"Oh my god…"

"Some of the boys really wanted out of the perimeter. Wanted to take them down is what they said. I headed them off before anyone could do anything. Figured that was your business."

"Where are they now?"

"The creatures are still outside. Just kind of wandering around out there. I'll admit, it's a mite unsettling."

"Yeah." I understand the meaning behind her words. "It's time for me to go."

She stands, brushing her hands against her jeans. "You're healing rather quickly. It's quite remarkable really. How are you feeling?"

"I haven't had a headache. Not like before."

"You should come out and eat with us. There's quail on the fire right now. Should be ready in about an hour."

"Okay, yeah. I'll be out in a little bit."

When I step out onto the porch, I spot the gaggle of girls over by the bonfire, scrappy teenagers not much younger than myself. The three of them glare at me with an abundance of vitriol.

A couple of women pull weeds over at the garden, glancing up now and then. Thorn walks out of the far woods with the water skins draped over his shoulders.

I pull the blanket around my shoulders, wanting to disappear into the shadows. The others approach him, each taking turns to fill their canisters.

"Come and eat," one of the women close to me says. I recognize her, but I can't remember her name. A tight smile rests on her face, but she gestures me toward the fire where a couple of birds spit and sizzle over the flames.

I follow with obvious hesitance, feeling as if I am walking to the gallows, the way everyone else keeps looking at me. The teenage girls never waiver in their hostile gaze. The man with the knife cuts a chunk of meat off the quail, lays it on one of the scraps of cloth, and hands it to me.

"We've also got some fruit," the woman says. "They found an orchard not far from here on the last supply run. Apples."

"Yeah, okay," I reply, unsure what else to say. She hands me one. The food tastes good and I eat without a care of the others.

Thorn approaches, having passed off the waterskins to one of the others. "You okay?"

"I feel like I haven't eaten in days." I pick clean one of the bones and toss it aside.

He chuckles. "You haven't really."

One of the girls suddenly points toward the gate, her eyes and mouth wide and frozen in horror. I turn to where she indicates, only to see the zombies standing in an unnaturally straight line, shoulder to shoulder, the space between them no more than about six inches.

The usual jerky shuffle has stopped. They just stand there,

each turned directly toward the farmhouse.

Almost immediately, Ezekiel appears at the door, seeking us out and rushing toward me. He holds something in his extended hand, something small.

"What are they doing?" he all but shouts, as he waves the item towards us. He glances back and forth between us and the zombies. "What are they doing?"

"They're standing still," Thorn answers. "Why are they standing still? What did you do, Eze?"

"I think I found the frequency. Watch." He jams his fingernail into some near-invisible slot in the device, twisting it. As he does, the creatures outside the fence suddenly break their odd formation, returning to their mindless shuffle.

"How did you do that?" I ask. "What is that thing?"

"This," he brandishes the device, which appears to be a small, coin-shaped item, "is what we pulled out of your head."

Thorn bristles. "Eze, what the hell…"

"No, it's okay," I say, leaning in to have a closer look. "I want to see it."

He hands me the item, cold in the palm of my hand. I peer at it, tracing the pad of my thumb over the matte black surface covered with tiny ridges.

Absently, my other hand reaches up to the back of my head, running lightly over the forming scar, already surrounded by a prickly new growth of my hair.

"This was in my head…" I murmur.

We stand in a circle, the three of us, staring down at the device in wonder.

"How does it work?" Thorn asks, tossing his head toward the zombies hovering outside the gate.

"So, check this out." Ezekiel pulls from his pocket a tiny screwdriver, just the right size to manipulate one of the ridges. He takes the disc, and presses, twisting it in a barely perceptible movement. Once again, the monsters stand stock still. "When I turn it here, they do this."

"What else can they do?" I ask.

"I don't know. I'll have to fiddle with it." He twists it again.

All of a sudden, a tightness consumes my head, as if a metal band is squeezing my skull. I press my fingers against my temples, shutting my eyes against the pressure.

"Whoa, what is it?" Thorn asks as he steadies my elbow.

"Is it one of your headaches?"

"No, it's different than that," I say. "I don't quite know."

"Oh my god," Fairlight says as she approaches. "Look."

On the other side of the fence, Penny stands facing towards us, the others haphazardly lined up behind her. Her decomposed face appears thin, gaunt, nothing more than a skull wrapped in a thin layer of skin.

The remarkable thing is her position, one hand lifted to her head, fingers extended, appearing to press into her temple. Her other arm is bent at a slight angle, at her side.

Her positioning mirrors my own, down to the minutest detail. When I lower my arm, she lowers hers. My arm, resting against Thorn's hand, carries the same angle as hers.

"Do something else," Ezekiel says, his lips twitching, eyes bright.

I lower my arms.

She lowers hers.

I step forward once.

She does too.

Her movements are not the herky-jerky motions of the undead. Rather, she carries herself with smooth motions, similar to those of the living.

"That's it," Ezekiel declares. "That's the frequency!"

"The what?" Fairlight asks.

"Upstairs, I had the thing tuned into the radio upstairs. It matches up with some of the channels, you see? Every time I switched it, I could connect it to one of the channels. That is, until I couldn't."

"What's that supposed to mean?" I ask.

"See, I happened to be able to see them out the window. When I turned it this last time, that's when the zombies went into the straight line. And just now, when we clicked it again, they started mirroring you."

"I'm still not sure I understand."

"The frequency somehow matches up with you."

"How can that be?" Fairlight shakes her head. "Frequencies? What are you saying?"

Ezekiel rolls his eyes, his enthusiasm slowing as he realizes the rest of us are just not as smart as him. "The human body puts off an electrical frequency, usually somewhere between sixty and seventy megahertz. This device, depending on the setting, emanates at various frequencies."

"And this is the frequency that connects me to them?" I ask.

"Yes. So it would seem."

"So, she was controlling me, with that thing in my head?"

"Perhaps. My theory is your headaches were caused when she adjusted the frequency from her location."

"I see."

"Look!" one of the teenage girls shouts, pointing toward the zombies, towards Penny. "Look! She's okay!"

Fairlight runs to the girl, grabbing her hands in hers and attempts to quiet her. "It's not what it looks like," she states firmly.

"Let her in!" the girl wails. "Let her in the gate! She's better now! Don't you see?"

The girl flails, fighting against Fairlight's grasp. Her friend attempts to console her, whispering small words. But the girl wrenches away, managing to escape and making a sprinting dash toward the gate.

Her youth and adrenaline give her enough speed that she gets ahead of everyone, slipping through the inner gate with relative ease.

"Penny, don't," I whisper.

Before anyone can stop the girl, she pulls open the outer gate, launching herself toward Penny. Ezekiel tries, but none of us can get to her fast enough.

I focus hard, doing my best to mentally push them back, to shield her from the monsters, but I am still too weak.

The girl rushes forward, her arms outstretched, her dark hair sticking to her tear-streaked cheeks.

As soon as she gets close enough to Penny, close enough to grab her up into her arms, she laughs, as one does returning to a long-lost friend. The sound erupts from her, a mix between crying and mirth and madness.

Penny bites into her neck, severing her artery immediately, blood erupting between her lips and the girl's neck. The girl dies laughing.

As soon as the blood hits the air, the other zombies frenzy, swarming them, laying into the two of them. They rip the girl to shreds before she even hits the ground. Nothing more than a corpse of blood and bones.

The other two stand watching from the inside of the fence, unable to stop the horror happening before them. The only remaining sound is the sickening crunching of flesh and the whimpering cries of the girl's two friends, fingers curled into the chain link.

One of them turns, seeking me out among the gathered few.

"You!" she shouts. "You're the one who brought them here. You made this happen! This is all your fault!"

My instinct wants to strike out at her, to lash out at the attack focused on me, but her words sink into me. She is not wrong.

All of this, not just Penny, not just the others, but all of it. The Fall of Humanity happened because of me. By the mere act of being born, coming into the world, the sequence of events leading to today would never have begun.

The virus would have died out, along with my mother. Perhaps Dr. Donovan would have tried to replicate it, but without my blood she would have failed.

She rants on as her remaining friend feebly attempts to pull her away. Fairlight and Ezekiel silently approach the girls, shepherding them away from me to the far side of the garden.

The girl finally collapses into her friend's arms, her rambling words giving way to grief-stricken weeping.

"She's right," I say.

"Ash, don't think like that." Thorn turns to me. I see a thin vertical line between his eyebrows.

"But she *is* right. I shouldn't have come here."

He shakes his head. "You had to. What about--?"

"Yeah, I got what I came for. Now it's time for me to go. That much is clear."

He falls silent, his eyes never leaving my face.

"Help Fairlight get everyone back over the mountains. Get them back to SeaHaven. I've got to finish this."

He reaches for me, tracing the back of his fingers along my cheek. As much as I want to lean into this feeling, I pull away.

"Don't. Just don't."

He does not respond. I make my way to the gate, feeling everyone's gaze on me. The gathered few are largely silent.

I don't turn back to look at any of them but keep my back turned as I open the gate. First one, then the other. When I turn to close the outer gate, I allow myself a quick glance, taking in the view of Fairlight, Ezekiel on the far right of the crowd, and

Thorn, over by the house, where I had left him alone, his eyes cast toward me with something akin to pity.

I close the gate with a loud metal clang.

I feel certain I will never see any of them again.

Twenty

We've been walking for three days, the land stretching out in all directions around us. I smell water close by.

It feels strange how my senses have increased with each passing day. Every morning I feel as if I have to do a sensory inventory just to see what I'm capable of.

I'm beginning to understand just how drawn these creatures are to their base needs, their ability to seek out fresh meat, living or dead. In a similar way, I find my own senses tweaking to my physical needs: water, heat, shelter, whatever food I come across.

Sometimes, the creatures closest to me mimic my movements if I am gathering firewood or shielding my eyes from the sun. They reach for phantom objects in front of them or lift a hand to their forehead, until I put my own down, all of us acting out this macabre salute.

Penny stays close by, now and then fading into the crowd, but always turning up again before much time goes by. The sun sits midway between the apex and the horizon by the time we reach the stream, not much more than a trickle across the edge of the plain, surrounded by small, twig-like trees.

"Okay," I say out loud, speaking to myself or to the creatures. I know they don't understand me, but speaking makes me feel better, at any rate. "This should do it. This is a good spot right here."

A few of them reply with the funny grunt sound they make sometimes. Perhaps nothing more than the air flowing through the decaying cavities of their throats.

I hang my backpack on the strongest of the tree branches closest to the stream, before leaning down to the water's edge. I scoop up handfuls to my mouth, refreshing and cold, drawing in as much as I can to pacify my thirst.

I also splash a bit on my arms and face. Glancing at the sun, I calculate we still have a good chunk of time before dark. Might as well try this out to see if it works.

"Okay, creatures," I say, turning toward my horde. "It's time for practice. Everyone ready?"

Their only response is blank stares and shuffling in place.

"Okay, let's give this a try."

First, I close my eyes, focusing my concentration. The connection feels slight at first, just a tickle around the edges of my mind.

I feel a resistance from them stemming from their animal selves, the void where humanity once lived. Within seconds, I feel their hunger, raging beyond understanding, a voiceless need which can never be quenched.

"There you are," I whisper.

Now I reach out just a little bit more, first strengthening the line between myself and the creatures closest to me. At first, the connection nearly overwhelms me, but I push past it.

One by one, they connect. To me, to each other. As the link grows and strengthens, we become a hive mind, equally yoked from where I stand to the far outer edges of the horde.

Their hunger becomes mine, and my drive propels their actions.

Softly I open my eyes with a slow, careful exhale. At the same moment, I am nearly knocked over by the breath of a thousand zombies.

Ah yes, I must remind myself to be careful of my actions if they are copying me.

I raise my right arm. They mirror me without hesitation. Lifting my left arm brings the same response.

I try different motions now, lifting one leg, then the other. Crossing my arms, bending at the waist. They all follow along, an assemblage of marionettes with tattered flesh and clothing fluttering against bones.

"Well alright then. Who wants to level up?" With this. I take out my blade, mainly just to have a grip on a weapon, swiping my arm out in front of me. as if fending off an attacker.

They follow the movement, each of them copying me down to the detail of my curved fingers. I place my knife back into the holster at my belt. They do so as well. Perfect. One more test.

With a quick motion, I flatten myself to the ground, keeping my eyes cut to the side to watch them. The dust settles around them. They look almost camouflaged against the ground.

Good. Exactly what I was going for.

This next step requires a bit of concentration, still feeling every tendril of their mental connection. I stand up, forcing my actions to remain separate from theirs, hoping against hope they remain where they are.

By the time I make it to my feet, I open my eyes, unsure of what I will see. I am met with the whole of the horde, lying on the ground just as I hoped.

"Excellent," I whisper.

Now I reach out once more. This time focusing on an individual. I find Penny, still there, somewhere toward the middle of the group.

I bid her to stand, just her. No one else. When I open my eyes, there she is in her yellow faded dress. From this distance, she almost looks just like a real girl. Between us, the rest of the horde remains lying, unmoving on the ground.

"Bingo! Good job, grunts," I say. "We'll pick this up again tomorrow."

Ever so carefully, I release the link between us all, leaving them to their mindless shuffling. Some of them wander off as I set up camp.

My curiosity gets the best of me once I'm done, and I decide to follow. I double-check the security of my camp, planted right up against the edge of the creek, not much more than a pile of rocks. Satisfied, I slip into the nearest cluster of creatures as they amble by.

Over the nearest hill, we find our way to a wandering pack of horses, healthy and untouched by the sickness. I think for a moment about Mare, feeling a twinge of sadness at her memory. Most likely, she is gone from this world by now. Perhaps I'll never know.

One of the horses had fallen, having broken its leg in a hidden gap covered in overgrown grass. It thrashed against the ground, the whites of her panicked eyes rolled toward the oncoming threat.

The zombies fall upon her without abandon, ripping flesh from her bones even as she screams against the pain. I stand back, letting them have their way, trying hard to ignore the cries of the dying creature, until, after far too many minutes, she falls mercifully silent.

I must do something to calm the gnawing of my own empty stomach. No squirrels or birds worth hunting had crossed my vision in days, one of the drawbacks of being the queen bee of a zombie horde, I guess.

I had seen the shell of a convenience store about a half a mile back, grown over with tendrils of vines. I had enough daylight to make it there and back.

If I admitted it, I could have joined them in feeding on that horse. The deep hunger had never gone away. Going to the convenience store was a conscious decision, one I made every moment of every day, for as long as I can remember.

The store is nothing more than three walls, a gaping hole where a glass door once stood. I step over shards of yellowed glass to get inside.

The fallen shelves appear bare. except for a few cans. Some kind of meat apparently. Cans are good. They last forever. I pile the few findings into my backpack. Luckily, these have the peel-back metal tab. The last one I open and scoop out the insides, careful not to cut my fingers against the sharp edges. A bit stale, but the boost of protein feels good to my depleted system.

Surrounded by these remnants of this fallen world, I wonder how they even survived as long as they did. All I see is shadows.

I can't help but recall the marketplace back at SeaHaven, how lively and vibrant the place seemed compared to this place. Satisfied with my haul, I tuck my pack over my shoulder and head back. Now that I'm away from the horde, I spotted a few birds here and there. But hunting takes time, and time is something I don't have.

When I return to camp, I find the horde spread out. They have stripped the poor horse down to the bones. The smell leaves a bit to be desired, but rotting flesh cannot be escaped in a world such as this. One gets used to it, I guess.

I start up the fire, waiting until it gets good and hot. The setting sun blazes the same color as the sparks floating into the twilight.

After my makeshift meal of roasted can-meat, I consider setting up my bed in the branches of the tree. But I glance around at my ragtag group of allies, aimlessly shuffling and occasional groans of misplaced air passing through rotting windpipes. They won't bother me. Of this I am certain.

My dreams fill the night with restless strangeness. A fire

consumes me, perhaps a foretelling of things to come. Even in the sleep-induced images of flames, I feel cold. Too cold.

I find myself running, someone is calling my name. Burning pieces fall all around me.

The dream shifts and I am a child sitting in the back of the car, speeding away from ground zero. The driver turns around to peer at me huddled in the back seat. The driver is now Simeon, grinning at me, as if nothing is wrong. The car is on fire, licking at the locked windows.

I bolt awake.

It is daylight.

I am safe.

The fire is nothing more than embers now. After I find a place to tuck away and relieve myself, I build up the fire once more.

The air has a pretty good morning chill, and the warmth is nice once the flames start kicking up. I dig a can of sardines out of my bag and eat them with my fingers.

"Okay, gang," I say, tossing the empty can into the flames. "Let's get to work."

After I rinse hands in the stream, splashing a bit of the cold water on my arms and face, I turn to face my horde. It takes a minute for me to engage the mental connection, but once I do, it all slips into place once more, tumblers in a lock, easy as anything.

All I ever sense from them is hunger. It reminds me of a character from a book I once read, ages ago, when I still lived in the library, but I could not remember the name. But I can tell the phenomenon only goes one way. I can feel them, but they cannot feel me.

I reach out, locating Penny in the center of the group and

nudge her to come closer to the front. What would I do with her, I wonder? Especially after the incident at the farm, the unrest which would never be resolved.

Whatever human had been called "Saffron" was now just an empty shell called Penny. She cannot feel. Not with her heart. Not with her body. It would be prudent for me to remember that in the days to come.

I put all this aside and relax my mind, letting the connection strengthen, flexing my mental web until we become a hive mind.

I beckon one of them towards me, once upon a time a young man. He wears a red baseball cap with some kind of writing on the front. Little white threads remain where the lettering once existed. I can't make out what it says.

He wears a once-white tank top with a button-up, short-sleeve shirt over it. I spot the name "Pete" embroidered on the left side of the shirt, just over the pocket. At some point his jaw had been broken, and the remaining bone hung at an awkward angle, making his face appear in a perpetual state of surprise.

He shuffles over to me, next to the fire. The others stay in place, shuffling in formation. I reach down and pick up a thick branch, partially burning from the fire.

"Okay, Pete. I'll need you to take one for the team now, buddy."

Averting my face, I place the burning end directly into the center of his torso, leaning hard into the motion to ensure the point of it sinks into his paper skin. He stumbles back, taking the burning log with him.

Within seconds, his torso lights up, flames laughing around his shoulders and face. The hat melts into his head and I turn away to try and escape the smell of burning flesh and hair.

It worked.

Pete has caught fire.

He stands still, a singular inferno. I focus my mind, stepping into his existence as he burns. He does not feel it, I realize. This is good. I don't think I could handle it if this process hurt them.

As he burns, I nudge him toward the creek, one foot in front of the other, stumbling on a root and launching face forward into the water.

"Okay," I turn to the others. "This looks like it might work."

I managed to get one or two more on fire, just to make sure I can replicate the results. Each time one of them perishes in the creek, I feel a tiny snuff as the last vestiges of their consciousness flickers out.

Penny shuffles in place, a wisp of her once-blonde hair drifts in an errant breeze. What kind of life might she have had if not taken by the doctor's goons? She and I could have been friends, perhaps in another life. "Don't worry, Penny. When this is over, I'll put you to rest." I step back to take in the view of the horde. "I'll put you all to rest. I promise."

I meant it. We still had a lot of training and testing to do before I took them to confront the doctor. But I had a pretty good idea of what was to come.

The thought of returning to SeaHaven was nothing more than a hypothetical at this point. But I knew one thing for sure. Between myself and Dr. Donovan, only one of us would be walking away.

Twenty-One

Dousing them in gasoline proves easier than I thought. Largely they ignore me as I move among them, splashing the acrid liquid around their shoulders and torsos, walking molotovs waiting for illumination. At least they won't feel any pain.

Not once do I take joy in the idea of facing Dr. Donovan again. The idea makes me sick to my stomach. This woman had raised me as her own, or so she claimed.

As much as she was capable, she had loved me. But her affections had always been nothing more than poison, a means to an end. My purpose in her life had always been as a killing machine. If she could not have me in that role, she would not stop until someone did it for her.

Every footstep brings us closer to the end game. The zombies walk along with me, feeling nothing of the trepidation within me.

All they feel is hunger. It never quite leaves them, regardless of how much they feed. This time, this one time, I hope it works in my favor.

Up ahead I spot the outer walls of the compound, recognizing the gaping hole from the day we liberated them. That was the day we lost Travis.

At least this time, there can be no lives lost.

Behind me, the creatures shuffle in place, keeping pace with my footsteps, stumbling into the fallen shelves and piles. Those who stumble are quickly replaced by the zombies behind them, filling in the gaps as deadly as the teeth of a shark.

The doorway to the hallway stands open, revealing darkness beyond. As soon as I step through, I see we are not alone.

Three zombies stand blocking my path toward the East wing. These creatures are different from the ones following me. They move in quick choppy motions, milky, seamy eyes, teeth chattering.

The middle one moves toward us with grasping, outstretched arms. He misses me as I step to the side, but not by much. The herky-jerky creature falls into the fray. Those behind me consumed him, ripping him to shreds with an unexpected vengeance.

The other two hang back, shuffling from one foot to another with unnatural movements. I make an attempt to connect my mind with them. I am met with a stabbing headache which pushes me to let go.

I can't read them.

That makes them dangerous.

With my right hand, I remove the knife from my belt. The canister of gasoline in my left hand, I slowly lower it down, tipping it forward to allow the contents to splash onto the ground between us.

With nothing more than a mental nudge, my zombies surge forward, flowing around me like water around a stone. I keep my eyes ahead, locked on the creatures in front of us.

The Herky-Jerkies backpedal, to no avail. Their awkward movements do not take them far before my horde overtakes them, finishing them off in a bloodbath.

We have the numbers in our favor, at least. I step forward, placing my feet carefully to avoid the black, viscus pools of blood on the floor and splashed against the walls.

Further down the hallway, I begin to get a vague recollection of where I am. Up ahead to the left would be the room in which I stayed.

The hallway veers, opening up to the right, which would lead to the elevators and the stairs, and, of course, the laboratories where I learned the truth of Dr. Donovan's work.

We move slowly in the darkness, making our way through the seemingly abandoned building. As we move forward, I let my mind go, giving myself over to the ever-present desire, the hunger which constantly flirts around the edges of my psyche.

Every moment I have spent among them has brought me a little bit closer to that part of me, but not until this moment, when I return to the place of my capture, do I accept the truth.

I am human.

And I am zombie.

Other than the undead horde walking step by step behind me, I am alone. So different from the first time I had been there. The place had been teeming with them, white coats scurrying up and down the halls, scritching at their clip boards, hanging on Dr. Donovan's every word.

Once we reach the open area in front of the laboratories, I pause. The sound of shuffling feet and guttural moans draws me back to the present.

I turn to face my undead. They seem to be waiting, as if their eyes are on me, seeking out some sort of direction from me, as impossible as that may be.

"Alright," I mutter. "Hold your horses. We've got to find the doctor first, okay?"

Blank stares from unblinking white eyes are the only response. The acrid scent of gasoline mingles with the dense odor of rotting flesh.

They part as I walk among them. I realize I feel something once again, the strange tickling in the back of my mind. I raise my hand absently, scratching at the skin at my hairline.

All at once, I realize what this is. I thought I was feeling

185

the call of the creatures, but here I am surrounded by them in close quarters.

If they were the cause, then I would be overwhelmed with it. I would be crouched in a corner, unable to move from the connection, from their pain. This feeling is something different, and I think I know what it is.

"I can find her," I say, addressing my undead army. "I know where she is. And when I find her, you will all be put to rest. That much I can promise you."

They follow me with their eyes as I move among them.

"I've always felt your pain," I continue. "I've always felt it. That constant hunger that never goes away, and that distant knowledge that the hunger will never go away. I'm going to set you free. And don't ever think I will forget your sacrifice today."

My gaze lands on Penny, a few steps from the front of the group. For a moment, I see her as she might have been, before she was taken from her life, kidnapped by Dr. Donovan's goons. I see her as a girl, only a bit younger than myself, not too different from myself had she had a chance to live.

She simply stares, as she always has.

I don't speak again. But I turn back to the lab doors. Dr. Donovan stands with her hands folded at her waist, surrounded by vials, Bunsen burners, beakers, piles of charts, and scribbled notes.

Her coat, once white, now appears dingy gray. Her hair had been pinned back into a low bun, but here and there, fly away hair stuck out in wiry, unkempt tendrils. Her face contains a wildness, a brokenness which I had not seen in her before I left here.

"Doctor Donovan," I say, evenly meeting her gaze.

Her eyes appear bright with madness as she smiles at me. "My prodigal child," she whispers. "I've been expecting you."

"What are you doing?" I ask. "What is this?"

She approaches me, arms extended, as if to give me an embrace, with a crazed grin on her face. I allow her to do so, taking in the details of her unkempt appearance, the dark matter under her nails, the acrid stench of her breath, and the sourness of sweat emanating from her body. She curls her arms around my shoulders, but I do not return the embrace.

"Oh, you've come back to me, Ashley."

"No, I've come back, but not for you. I'm here to end this."

"Oh, no, no, no!" She takes my hands in hers, cold and clammy. "You don't understand. I did this for you, Ashley. All of this, for you. I found a way to make everything better for you. To make a world where you would fit. Where everyone would be like you. Come and see." She scurries over to the cabinet, picking up a vial filled with a bright blue liquid. She holds it out in front of her, as if presenting a prize. "Look, here it is. We've already tested it so many times."

"How?" I ask. "How have you tested it?"

"In the early trials, we used horses."

"Why horses?"

"They have the closest genetic makeup to humans related to the other animals in this area."

That explains where Mare came from. "And?"

"And we have found the ability to manipulate the very DNA of the living."

"Dr. Donovan," I say. "How many of you are left? Who helped you with this?"

She laughs, her mouth extended into a ghastly grin. "There's no one left," she replies. "That's how I knew you would come back to me."

With these words, she reaches for a syringe from the prep

station, filled with the same blue liquid and already affixed with a hollow needle.

"Doctor, no!" I reach for her, but my feet move in slow motion. She is too far away. She plunges the needle into her arm, directly into a vein suppressing the plunger before I reach her. I catch her, just as her knees buckle.

"Now I'll be just like you," she whispers.

"What did you do? What's in the syringe?"

Her face becomes ashen as I cradle her head in my lap. "It's you, Ashley," she says in a weak, shallow voice. "This is the serum I was able to draw from your blood. I gave it to them. I made them like you, so you would have a place to come back to, a place to belong."

My view grows blurry as tears fill my eyes. As much as my rage burns inside me, her words cut me to the core. Her body convulsed, her eyes rolling back in her head, teeth clenched. All I can do is steady her, until she calms once more.

"Ashley," she says as her mad eyes search wildly around the room.

"Here. I'm here," I choke out the words, overcome with anger and sadness, threatening to consume me.

"Ashley, I want to tell you…"

"Okay, yes. What is it?" I say. Whatever it is, I don't want to hear it, but it is unclear if she will survive the injection. Already, I see a blueness creeping into her lips and around her eyes.

"I want you to know," she continues in a rasping voice. "I want to tell you about your mother. May I tell you?"

I do my best to suppress an audible wail at the mention of my mother. "Fine," I whimper, nothing more than placating a madwoman.

"She wanted you."

"What?" Tears stream from my eyes.

"She wanted you so much. That's why she signed up for the experiment. She couldn't afford any care for you otherwise. Of course, we didn't know about you at first. She had already been through the first series of injections. When she started showing symptoms, she came to me and told me about the pregnancy. By then it was too late."

Once more her body seizes, her back arching against the cold laboratory floor.

"Doctor!" I shout, rocking her in an attempt to revive her.

Her eyes clear, returning their focus back to me.

"At the end, she made me promise…" Her voice cracked, breaking up her words. "She made me promise to save you. To take care of you."

"How far?" I ask. "Before she turned. How far along was she before she turned?"

"Six months," the doctor replies. "You were perfect when we got you out. Just perfect, all pretty and pink. The perfect little girl. The other doctors wanted to… dispatch you, but I had made a promise to keep. And I intended to keep it."

"What would have happened?" Tears stream down my face, landing in little splashes on my fingers.

"They wanted to study you, dissect your body. But when I looked into your face, your perfect, pink little face, I knew I had to save you."

"Is that what you did?" I say in a choked voice, my whole body trembling with unspent emotion. "You saved me? The closest thing you did was keep me alive. But you didn't save me. How do you justify the childhood you gave me? Making me walk through rooms full of zombies when I was no more than a child! You didn't save me any more than you saved my mother. You made me as much of a test subject as any of the other scientists

189

would have done. Don't fool yourself into thinking you treated me any better. You didn't save me at all!"

"Ashley, I did. And I always knew you would come back to me." With these words, she convulses once more in my arms, so hard that her body lurches out of my grasp onto the floor.

Her skin is now fully blue, spreading outward from the injection site on her arm, the veins beneath popping out against the flesh on her arms and the base of her neck. Her body shakes so violently I can hear the sound of her head hit the hard floor with a loud crack. It is time to go.

"The beacon," I say desperately, trying to reach her before it is too late. "Doctor, where is the beacon?"

She turns toward me, still in control of her faculties, for whatever that means. The grin across her face bears the stamp of madness.

"The beacon, Doctor!"

With one trembling hand, she points to the computer console at the far end of the counter. Leaving her convulsing on the floor, I hurry to the console, glancing at the controls, a series of one word controls and a screen perched over a keyboard.

Scanning the words, I find one labeled "home." I return my gaze to the doctor, still quaking on the floor. Squeezing my eyes closed, I flip the switch.

"Ashley," she calls, her voice distant and weak. I make my way to her, trying to steady her to her feet.

"Come with me," I say. "Come back with me. We could use a doctor at SeaHaven."

"I won't leave, Ashley," she whimpers, even as her body continues to shake. "I won't leave my work."

"Doctor please. It's time to go now," I cry once more, but I know she is already lost. I pull on the lapel of her lab coat, trying again to get her to her feet. "Come on, we have to go now."

With one last flash of clarity, she meets my gaze, offering a languid grin. "They won't hurt us, Ashley," she says with eerie calm. "They won't."

The creatures outside the laboratory doors, drawn by the beacon, press their way through, quickly filling the small space with their acrid stench. I have no choice. I leave her leaning against the doors of the counter.

As I exit the room, I scoop up the handle of the half-empty gasoline canister, push past the zombies, through the door and into the hall leaving a trail of liquid behind me.

At the top of the hall, I pause. The creatures still push past me, as if I am not there, not even attracted by the rattle of the matchbook I pull out of my pouch.

"I'm sorry, Mother," I say, before I drop the lit match to the floor.

The flames surge forward with a rush of heat, catching the feet of those closest to me. One by one, they erupt in flames, still shoving forward toward the call of the beacon, pieces of burning flesh falling in their wake.

I don't have much time. The zombies behind me had not yet caught, but it was only a matter of seconds, the way we had come already clogged with more approaching undead.

I take the stairs two at a time, making my way for the level below. Hopefully, the path to the front door remains clear. Behind me, gasoline catches and spreads, crackling, rushing, roaring. I run toward the front doors, feeling the heat building up at my back.

For just a moment, I connect once more, allowing myself to see through their eyes peering down at the Doctor, surrounded in orange and blue flames. Her hair had turned stark white, her eyes milky gray, and still she smiles.

I run, pushing with all my might to get to the front gate

before the fire consumes the weight-bearing parts of the building.

Just as I clear the door, engulfed in clean, cold air, the explosion pushes me forward, sending me tumbling onto the rocky ground.

All around, zombies arrive, called by the pulse of the beacon. For every creature arriving, I feel others slip away as they perish in the fire, releasing the connection to my mind like a clipped thread.

I scramble to my feet, ignoring the sting on the palms of my hands where I landed and quickly moving to a safe distance, turning to watch the inferno.

There are thousands of them, all shuffling toward the flaming edifice like moths to a flame. I spot one, standing outside the edge of the fire, close enough to illuminate what's left of her features.

Penny.

She stands facing away from the flames, standing in contrast to the rest of them marching, marching, marching toward the fire.

"Go," I whisper. "Go and be at peace."

Even from this distance, I feel her connecting to my mind, seeking me out among the chaos. This is how I can feel the beacon calling her, controlling her body. She is fighting against it, even in her decayed state.

"Go!" I say out loud, willing the same thought to her in my mind. "There is nothing left for you here!"

She stands, unmoving, while the others walk around her. Most of them catch right away when they reach the heat of the fire. Others smolder in a slow burn, until they are no more.

Finally, finally, Penny turns away, dropping her gaze and walking toward the fire. With a final lurching step, she disappears into the amber inferno.

I stay with her for as long as I can, keeping our mental connection open, seeing the fire through her eyes. As I cling to the damp ground, I feel the heat surrounding her, my cheeks burning as I am the one walking into the pyre.

When I close my eyes, her surroundings come into focus through a milky sheen in my mind's vision. She follows the others, shoulder to shoulder with her kin, snaking down the hallways, around corners, deeper into the burning building.

Fire leaps along the remaining walls, across the ceiling, ahead, behind.

Everything burns.

Penny walks onward, drawn by the beacon. Her yellow dress catches fire as the flames reach her. The end comes quickly then, as her body succumbs to the heat.

Burning flesh, bones, yet still she moves forward. I feel her mind dissolve at the end, one moment heat, hunger, desire.

The   next,   nothing.

Penny is gone.

Through it all, she felt no pain.

I cling to the connection for as long as I can, lying there in the cold grass, the night's dew already falling upon me, trying to find an absolution in the void left by her absence.

I find none.

There is nothing left to do but to wait for the fire to burn itself out.

Twenty-Two

They had vacated the farm, hopefully returning to SeaHaven as I had suggested. Maybe, just maybe, Fairlight's group can integrate into the community there. Hopefully, she and Clarice won't clash too much. The thought makes me chuckle.

My first instinct is to walk the perimeter, checking the fencing for any kind of breech and finding none.

"Good job, Ezekiel," I whisper.

Next, I make my way to the tree beyond the garden, broken bones reaching for the sky.

The sight of the graves calms me, two small stones with their names burnt onto each of them. I sit directly between them, crossing my legs and placing my palms against the cold ground.

"One more time," I say, "I wish I could have seen you just one more time." I move my hand to the bare earth over Eden's grave. "I don't know what to do right now, Eden. I just don't know. Everything seems so simple to everyone else. Live. Breath. Survive. Sleep. Repeat." At first, I don't notice the dampness on my cheeks, not until the tears fall onto the dirt around my fingers.

"I want to be like them, but I'll always be different. I'm not one of them. I don't belong there." I had never said these words out loud before. It feels strange but somehow freeing. "The truth is, I'm lying to them. I'm lying to myself for ever thinking I could have a normal life. Everything I've ever done has just been play acting at having a normal life." I glance up at the setting sun, blazing the sky with blood. "I don't know if I should go back," I whisper, my voice betraying my emotion.

A sound interrupts me, a low, ghostly moan just beyond the fence. When I look up, I see Mare, standing there, watching me with her milky eyes.

She tosses her head, like any horse would, except a chunk of flesh falls off her ear as she does, exposing the skull beneath. Her legs have decayed to the bone with thin strips of flesh fluttering in the breeze. She appears top heavy, despite her ribs showing through the sagging skin around her torso.

"Where did you come from?" I say. She only responds with her strange ghostly whinny. I stand up and brush the dirt off my jeans. "You're looking like you've seen better days, my friend."

When I walk over to the gate, she follows me, shadowing my steps along the fence, twenty feet and two fences separating us. I make sure to close the inner gate behind me before I let her into the causeway. I don't want to take any chances.

"Hey, Mare," I murmur, opening the gate to let her through. "Where you been, girl? Why'd you follow me back here? Huh?"

Her presence feels in some strange way like an answer to the question. Leave it to Eden to find a way to send me a zombie horse from the great beyond.

I don't know if riding Mare will be the best option. She is not in any shape to bear the weight of a human being. She can carry a pack, though. I head back toward the farm, leaving her for a moment in the grassy spaces between the fences.

From the panic room, I collect the medical kits, the dried meats and fruits, and as much of the canned goods as I am able to carry, piling everything into the saddle bags. Dragging it back to her takes some doing, and the heaviness of it makes me grateful for the presence of the horse. She takes the weight with relative ease, stepping her feet slightly wider to distribute the weight.

"There we go," I say, finding a dry spot on her nose, the skin there shriveled and emaciated, sinking into the skull. Only a fist-sized patch of fur remains. This is the only place I can pet her without getting gunk all over my hand.

"We've still got a lot of daylight, Mare. Are you ready to make a trip?"

After another circle of the property, we exit out the gates once more. I follow the road, the same way we had always gone. I realize, every time I leave this place, I think it's the last time.

This time it feels certain though.

The creatures roam the landscape in the distance, still following the fiery beacon in the distance. I can't escape the idea that some small part of me is still controlled by the beacon, just as they are, the part of that is like them.

But ever since Ezekiel had done whatever he had done to my headaches, I had to admit the pull was not as strong. Almost as if he had reset my frequency to something different, not quite undoing the damage done, but at least making me unreachable by Dr. Donovan.

"But she's dead, isn't she," I say out loud, as if Mare had some concern about the issue. "I left her writhing on the floor of a burning building."

We walk for nearly a day and a half, the full moon providing enough light for us to keep going. Mare could have gone on endlessly, but I at least still required rest. Finally, we stop to make camp deep in the mountains.

Mare lays down on the grassy patch next to the stream, her breathing sounding more wheezy. She had not slowed down at all during the journey. I leave her to rest at the water's edge while I rifle through the bag, looking for something that might suffice as a meal for her.

Finally, I settle on the jerky, hand feeding her bits of the meat while I eat the dried fruit. Her breathing steadies. I know it is no more than a reflex of her body. She has no need of oxygen, just like the rest of the undead.

I curl up next to her, comfortable in the knowledge that we are the only two sentient creatures on the mountainside, living or otherwise. The ground is dry, and we have a good water source. A different time and I could have made a permanent camp here.

Eventually, I drift off to sleep, lulled by the quiet sounds of Mare lying next to me.

The sound of the stream rushing along beside us wakes me, sunlight filtering through the leaves, creating dappled shadows all around us. I lean over, cupping my hands to pull some water to my lips.

My next order of business, inspired by the sound of the water, is to locate a place to relieve myself. I tuck behind a tree a good distance from the stream.

"Okay, Mare. It's time to go." I return to her prone body and place one hand gently on her emaciated flank. I feel hardly any movement, but it does not concern me. She is, after all, already dead.

She lifts her head, what's left of her ears twitch in my direction.

"What's wrong, girl? What's the problem?" I do my best to sound comforting. She lays her head back down on the ground, her rib cage heaving up and down in a charade of breathing, a hollow rattle emanating from the cavity. Her rate of decay is such that some of the skin had fallen off during the night. Her journey has come to an end.

The following hours pass by with exhausting brutality, waiting for her to fade away. I stay with her, feeling the remaining energy draining from her body.

It takes such a long time, this kind of death. Giving her a mercy killing would be pointless, since I'd probably miss her cerebellum altogether. Plus, I don't know enough about horse brains to figure out where it is.

This kind of death is brutal to watch. The undead persons are one thing, but animals are innocent. They do not deserve this, any of it.

Now and then, I whisper quiet words of comfort. It feels strange, because she is already dead, just a remnant, the last dregs of an empty vessel.

By the time the sun sets, Mare is gone.

No big dramatic moment. No gasping or struggling for life, just… gone.

I stay for another few moments, waiting for the darkness to settle in. As twilight deepens, I take the time to cover Mare's body with leaves and dirt, as I don't have the resources to properly bury her. It won't take too much time for her to disappear back into the ground forever.

I take my time in relocating the contents of the saddle bag into my backpack, managing to get nearly everything. The bag feels quite heavy still. If I have to choose, I would take the medical supplies. SeaHaven has plenty of food, but I am not there yet, and who knows what might happen in the meantime.

Traveling through the night and the following day consists of not much more than walking, resting, checking the sky, and more walking. At times, I consider taking off on my own, to go back to living off the land just like I used to do. SeaHaven can go on without me. That much is certain.

But then I think about Thorn. And Alma. Her child and Marcus. They are growing up in a world which no one has seen before.

I reach the edge of the city before dusk of the following day. The silence of the concrete structures belies the slight lift of hope I feel at returning to the community, the bustle of people, smiles, living faces. It still surprises me how quickly I had become so accustomed to this kind of life.

When I round the bend to the parking lot, I am greeted by the goatherder and his large herd. He offers a wave and a hearty greeting, still guiding the animals with the large, thin stick, leading them to the inland grasses for grazing. In the distance, I see the bright blue line of the ocean horizon against the pale sky.

Among the activity of people, I spot Rose at the water's edge. She has her fishing line set up. Someone calls my name from the other direction, prompting Rose to turn around.

"Ash!" She waves wildly, lowering the fishing line to the post before taking off towards me. I wave back and pick up my pace, setting down my weapon and backpack.

The tiredness from travel lightens for a moment. What is that feeling of lightness? Is this what people refer to as hope?
She grabs me up in a hug, quickly followed by the embrace of others in the community, Clarice, Simeon, Alma. Children come running from their places along the beach, abandoning their schooling for the day. All of this is common practice for the return of any citizen. Cheers and cacophony surround me, overwhelming me.

"You're okay!" Rose exclaims. "I'm so glad you're okay!"

"Where is Thorn?" I ask.

"He's out hunting. He'll be back soon. He's going to be so happy to see you."

Clarice steps in, placing her hands around my shoulders to shield me a bit from the pressing crowd. "Alright everyone. Ash is probably tired. Let us leave her to rest while we prepare the evening feast."

The mention of food brought another round of cheers, but the hubbub relaxed enough to allow Rose and I to make our way down the beach toward the fire.

"You must be exhausted," she said. "Come on. We've already got some food on the fire."

I don't notice the soreness in my muscles until I settle down, sitting on the sand. Rose hands me a portion of roasted shark meat, white, flaky, and cooked just right. She places it on a large green leaf, nestled in with cut bits of baked apples.

I eat without pausing to answer her barrage of questions. Rose can wait. I am back. That's all that matters right now.

"There's plenty of fish in the sea, you know, Ash," Rose says with a chuckle.

Finally, I feel sated enough to give her my attention. "The others made it back?"

"Yes," she says. "About a week ago. Ezekiel and Fairlight came back with the others. They're around somewhere, out on their daily rounds, I'm sure."

"I'm glad they made it. How is everyone adjusting?"
She laughs again, and I realize how much I missed the absolute light which shines from her. That and the full stomach have considerably lifted my spirits. I reach for the backpack, gesturing for Clarice, to show her the supplies I brought from the farm.

"I think there's someone who wants to see you," she says in her rich accent, which sounds like warm honey. I glance in the direction she points and spot Marcus down the beach, staring out over the water. The sight of him makes my chest ache.

"Has he spoken since I left?"

"Not yet," Clarice says, "but he's watched for you. Every day he waited by the road. If he's not there, he's staring out at the water. You should go. I don't think he knows you're here yet."

I stand up, making my way out of the gathering by the fire. He has never been the huggy type, but he would get one from me today. I trot towards him with a smile on my face.

"Hey you," I say, leaning down and scooping him into my

arms. He does not pull away, but leaves his arms hanging slack at his sides. I barely notice as he takes a breath I am too caught up in the joy of having him back, of being back.

"They're coming," he whispers against my shoulder.

I don't realize at first the voice is his, so soft and quiet, stilled from the months of disuse. I pull back, looking into his face, unsure of what I have just heard. "Marcus… Did you…?"

He nods, his voice stronger this time. "They're coming."

"Oh, Marcus," I reply. "No. They're not coming here. I stopped them. We're safe, Marcus. We're safe."

He turns toward the water, holding the same stoic expression as he ever has. I follow his gaze out over the gently lapping water. Across the breaking waves, I see a distant ship shining against the horizon. The islanders, perhaps coming again to bring us coffee and pineapples.

"Well how about that, Marcus?" I whisper, draping an arm around his shoulder. "Looks like we're going to have a feast tonight after all."

I stand, taking his hand in mine. Together we walk along the wet sand back toward Clarice and the others, back to the fire pit to share with them the good news. I only hope Thorn returns soon. I can't wait to see him.

End

Reviews for Rising Ash

"This is a lovely story full of nice vivid imagery. Westerman has a smooth, well developed style and everything clipped along at a good pace. The scene setting/world building is good - make that great - rich and evocative, dropping me right into the world. Quite a feat for an indie author ... "

-Lindsey Williams, *Motherhood*

"...Ash herself is a tough and resourceful character with a mysterious past. It left me wanting to read more!"

-Katherine Bryant, *Branna's Song: The Coldwood Saga*

"I find Ash to be an interesting character. She presents as a tough and savvy zombie hunter as she goes in search of stuff. In this book, what that constitutes the stuff is not revealed in its entirety. It is known that some of the stuff has to do with Ash's past. However, there are hints that Ash has another side to her."

-Stacy Overby, *Ambrosia: A Poetry Anthology*

About the Author

R.G. Westerman has been writing nearly her whole life and has a number of short stories available on Amazon through various anthologies. She loves to explore and create stories about problems she will never have, such as oncoming zombie hordes and other creatures of the fantastic!

When not creating tales of horror and whimsy, R.G. can be found hiking the mountain trails of Appalachia. She occasionally dabbles in freelance and endures her fabulous day job. She currently lives in picturesque Central Kentucky with her husband and two genius children. Rising Ash is her first published novel.